*. . . I rem . . . . he
Time Tra . . . . he
second, ... r,
story, a . . . . d
Photographs he would bring
with him.*

*But I am beginning to fear now
that I must wait a lifetime for
that. The Time Traveler vanished three years ago. Up to the
present he has not returned . . .*

So ended H. G. Wells' immortal science fiction
classic, THE TIME MACHINE. Since it was
written, millions of readers have wondered what
happened to the Time Machine and its inventor
. . . waiting for that "second, perhaps still strang-
er, story." But the wait is over.

A sequel to THE TIME MACHINE exists!
Here is the story of the man who succeeded in
establishing communication with the Time Traveler's closest confidant and who finally learned
the astonishing events that followed the Time
Machine's second long trip into the future.

An exciting science fiction event, DAW
Books is proud to present its first publicly
available English language edition.

The Return of the Time Machine

by
EGON FRIEDELL

Translated by
Eddy C. Bertin

DAW BOOKS, INC.
DONALD A. WOLLHEIM, PUBLISHER
1633 Broadway, New York, NY 10019

FIRST PRINTING 1972

 DAW TRADEMARK REGISTERED
U.S. PAT. OFF. MARCA
REGISTRADA. HECHO EN U.S.A.

PRINTED IN U.S.A.

Dedicated to my
genial fellow actor
Max Gülstorff

Table of Contents

Editor's Introduction:

H. G. Wells And Egon Friedell

Although H. G. Wells was to devote his lifetime to writing, his first published novel, *The Time Machine,* may remain his single finest work of creation. This would be due to many special factors.

It was his first literary creation; he had been writing different versions of it since his school days, changing and developing his thoughts. It was therefore of all his work the longest in gestation (if perhaps among the shortest of his novels) having undergone this long series of metamorphoses. By the time it was published in its final form, in 1895, it had become his most polished literary product. A gem of a novel it still is and it still remains—and it has gone into edition after edition and translation after translation through the length of the Twentieth Century without losing any of its fascination.

Again, it held a concept which shook its readers. The social vision—that of humanity ultimately dividing into two distinct species—the Morlocks descended from the working class and the Eloi descended from the "leisure class." Both class concepts derived from the oversimplified picture of the social scene of the Industrial Nineteenth Century as viewed by its most alarmed and morbid reformers. The passage of eight hundred thousand years had finalized the class fission in an evolutionary sense, for the Morlocks had become a nocturnal underground race of humanoid carnivorous "rats" while the Eloi had evolved into a sort of never-maturing innocent race of bipedal "sheep."

Not a pleasant picture, no matter what your viewpoint.

Then there was the whole theory of time travel. It had been speculated upon before, but Wells put it into the clearest terms, speculating on time as a dimension like length and breadth and width in which movement could be made back and forth— and hence a machine could be invented to traverse it, even as the air would shortly be subjected to scientific conquest (the invention of the airplane was on the order of the day and there was endless speculation about it during the last decades of the previous century).

The impact of both concepts in that finely polished novel launched Wells' career. The book also left its readers hungry for a sequel. The further adventures of the Time Traveler was implied by his disappearance with his machine at the end of the book. The anonymous narrator, one of the small circle who had been privileged to hear the story from the inventor's own lips, arrives at the last only to witness the disappearance of the Traveler and his machine. As he tells it:

> . . . I remained waiting for the Time Traveler, waiting for the second, perhaps still stranger story, and the specimens and photographs he would bring with him.
>
> But I am beginning to fear now that I must wait a lifetime for that. The Time Traveler vanished three years ago. Up to the present he has not returned. . . And so, ending in a kind

of dead wall, the story of the Time Machine must remain for the present at least.

To the best of my knowledge, as a science fiction reader and collector, I had not heard of any effort to write a sequel, to write the follow-up that the cliffhanger ending so clearly demanded. Wells himself certainly had no intention of doing so. Though thousands of science fiction stories have been written since 1895, I had not encountered any that purported to be a sequel until I discovered a copy of a book in a Munich antiquarian shop entitled, *Die Reise mit der Zeitmaschine* by Egon Friedell. This, now retitled in English, *The Return of the Time Machine,* is the work you now hold in your hand.

Who was Egon Friedell and by what right did he presume to take up the Time Traveler's tale where Wells left off?

It turns out that Egon Friedell, a Viennese literateur and dramatist, was a writer whose work in many ways paralleled that of H. G. Wells, and who can justifiably be termed a contemporary of Wells save in the language in which he worked. H. G. Wells was born in 1866, Friedell on January 21, 1878. It must have been as a student that Friedell first read *The Time Machine*—the same sensitive period of life in which Wells had created it. Friedell's first published work, a philosophical dissertation, appeared in 1904, followed over the years by a variety of other books and culminating in 1927 and 1932 by his three volume *Cultural History of Modern Times,* which can be compared with similar philosophical and historical studies done by Wells himself in about the same period. Friedell was working on his *Cultural History of Ancient Times* (the first volume of which was published in Vienna in 1936) when his work was interrupted by the seizure of Austria by the Nazis. Friedell, of Jewish descent, committed suicide on March 16, 1938.

After the occupation of Germany at the end of the war, it was this hitherto unpublished sequel to *The Time Machine* which was the first work of Friedell's to return his name to print. It was published in a small edition in 1946, by R. Piper & Co., in Munich, under U.S. Army Military Government License. H. G. Wells died August 13, 1946, but he may have been alive at the time it appeared.

When was it written? In their comment on the author the German publishers remark only that Friedell had placed the manuscript in their hands. They do not say when but presumably after it had become impossible to publish it under the Hitler regime. There is no clue as to its actual date of writing. The text carries one implication that could date it in the Twenties—if so, why had it not been published at that time? Or could it have been written late in Friedell's life, too late to get it into print. Or could it be that Egon Friedell wrote the work because, like so many readers, he felt that *The Time Machine* needed a sequel—and then, having written it, simply put it away abashed at having written what a greater writer than himself had not attempted?

Did Friedell ever write to H. G. Wells? The book opens with a letter purporting to be from one author to the other. Wells, according to the novel, did not answer though his secretary did. Is all that fiction or is part of it, Friedell's initial letter, an actuality? Did Wells ever have a secretary by that name and would she have dared reply as she did?

Before undertaking the translation of this work, a letter was written to the H. G. Wells Society in England asking the above questions. No reply was ever received. Yet, during a recent visit to London, your editor had a brief talk with an official of that society, the science fiction writer William F. Temple, and it was admitted that the inquiry had been received and that the Society knew of this project. But then why no answer? Possibly there is no record of any Wells correspondence with Friedell. Yet it is unlikely that Wells was unaware of Friedell's cultural histories so similar to his own.

In addition to his literary creations, Friedell was well known in Vienna as an actor, dramatist and critic. He had translated Carlyle and Macaulay, adapted the works of many classical writers, and achieved fame for his ironic aphorisms and essays. Since the publication of *Die Reise mit der Zeitmaschine* in its one edition in 1946, several of his books have come back into print in Austria and Germany, and he is regaining prestige. In 1971, Claasen Press of Hamburg published Peter Haage's book about Egon Friedell and his circle, entitled *Der Partylöwe der nur Bücher Frass*, or, as we would translate it: *The Party Lion That Only Devoured Books*.

Here then is the only known book-length direct sequel to *The Time Machine* in its first translation into English. The Party Lion may have been a terror to the authors of Vienna but here he pays tribute to his own inspirer.

It is interesting to note his attempts to name those who viewed the original Machine's takeoff. Wells himself preferred to call his characters merely the Time Traveler, the Medical Man, the Editor, the Very Young Man, and so forth, naming only one, Filby, and that admittedly a disguise. In some of the earlier versions of Wells' incompleted drafts names do appear. In the version entitled *The Chronic Argonauts*, the Time Traveler is named as a Dr. Moses Nebogipfel and his closest confidant is a

Reverend Elijah Cook. Friedell's effort to learn the real names of the Traveler and his circle must be ascribed to a curiosity that probably bothered him since his student days. But, if we can take the book at its word, perhaps he did ferret out the real names of the people who were present that fateful day when the Time Traveler set out for the sunset of the world.

Unless we build our own time machines some day, we shall never know how much of Friedell's novel was known and allowed by H. G. Wells or whether it was ever, in any sense, an approved work. We shall therefore make no such claim. It remains nonetheless as unique in its own way as the original novel.

—D.A.W.

Author's Introduction:

An Extraordinary Correspondence*

1

To Mr. H. G. Wells, London.

Vienna, February 3rd, 1908

Much respected Master!

An enchanted admirer—more: a real devourer of your various works—takes the risk to ask you a modest question, which, he hopes, won't take too

*Author's footnote: The reader can't help but notice (in observing what follows here) that several people seem to suffer from a strange disease: they are completely unable to stick to their subject. The reason for this can be found in the fact that these are all people belonging to what can be called the "mind profession." It is well-known that this breed is different from the everyday man, as it has an astounding inability to concentrate on one subject. One could almost say that this is the most distinctive mark of all "mind workers," no matter if they are poets, psychics possessing the "sense of eternity," actors, journalists or raconteurs. While engaging in story-telling, they all always leap from the hundreds into the thousands. As a consciously objective reporter, however, I feel obliged to present this exchange of letters as a complete unity, just as it really happened. There may be someone who thinks these opinions—which, I admit, often must resemble idle ramblings—are as much out of place as I think they are myself. Please: he should feel absolutely free to pass over this introduction as quickly as possible, and to go on with the bulkier but more substantial food, which is presented in the narrative of the adventures and accidents of the hero in the later parts of this book.

much of your time. In your marvelous novel *The Time Machine,* which appeared some time ago, you have written about a scientist who invented a machine with which he could travel through the Fourth Dimension, this one being Time itself. The scientist first tried it forward, into the future, and you have spun out his adventures there with such a poetical imagination that surely they must delight everyone who reads them. He returned to tell his companions in the present everything which happened to him; but then soon remounts his machine to start a journey into the past . . . and there the novel ends. You finish with:

"The Time Traveler vanished three years ago. And as everybody knows, he has never returned. One cannot choose but wonder. Will he ever return? It may be that he was swept back into the past, and fell among the blood-drinking, hairy savages of the Age of Unpolished Stone; into the abysses of the Cretaceous Sea; or among the grotesque saurians, the huge reptilian brutes of the Jurassic Times. He may even now—if I may use the phrase—be wandering on some plesiosaurs-haunted olitic coral reef, or beside the lonely saline lakes of the Triassic Age."**

Now, however, quite a few years have passed since the publication of your novel. During this time I have often and intensely thought and worried about this journey into the past. In my humble opinion there can be only two possibilities.

Either: Your narration contains more than a few

**Author's footnote: These parts out of Wells' novel *The Time Machine* are not to be found in the German edition available in our book stores, but are newly translated from the original edition. The correspondence also has been translated, as everything was of course written in English. Mr. Wells does not know German, which may well be the only quality he has in common with the translator of his book.

grains of truth. In this case it is highly possible that in the meantime you have heard again from this very special man.

Or: The story is a completely free invention of your genial pen. This being so, why then do you hesitate so long to continue this story, which after all is only dependent on your own volition?

Everything seems to indicate that this last version is correct, even the behavior of the Time Traveler himself, and even more of those surrounding him. The Time Traveler once said: "To tell you the truth . . . I hardly believe it myself," and another phrase: "No. I cannot expect you to believe it. Take it as a lie . . . or a prophecy. Say I dreamed it in the workshop. And, taking it as a story, what do you think of it?" And the editor, Mr. Blank (who seems to be the most intelligent and serious-minded of the group) answers with a sigh, "What a pity it is you're not a writer of stories," and on the way home explains it all as "a gaudy lie." The journalist, a serious, timid, bearded man, who hasn't opened his mouth during the whole evening (a pity you kept his name a secret, as well as that of the Time Traveler), cloaks himself in silence, thereby conveying so much more than with words.

But suppose that there *is* indeed a Time Traveler, something which after all is still possible, and suppose he *did* make a journey through time—which seems quite unlikely to me after all that I've written earlier in this letter—then you have the obligation to make public everything which you have learned of him since then. If you haven't learned anything new, at least you should make this known. It is a simple duty to your countless readers and admirers, among whom I belong.

Yours very respectfully,
Egon Friedell.

P.S. I'd like to use this opportunity to ask you for an autograph. But please, not just a simple signature, but a beautiful and perhaps long sample of your writing which hasn't appeared in print yet.

2

To Mr. Egon Friedell, Vienna.

London, February 11, 1908.

Dear Sir!

Your hopes have greatly deceived you. Mr. Wells, in whose name I'm writing to you, does feel that your letter is "too much trouble." In fact he thinks you are far from being modest." Is there indeed anything more presumptuous (being a woman, I won't use a stronger expression for it, though I'm greatly tempted to) than trying to snoop into concealed mysteries, and masking this under a cloak of admiration? I won't even mention the absolutely tasteless tone you've taken! Because even those thoughtless and exaggerated phrases such as "admirable imagination," "genial invention" as well as other similar ones, that you've used so freely in connection with Mr. Wells, can only be received as rude and provocative insults to him. Even if they haven't been dictated by malicious intent—which in your own interest, I hope is the case—you are nonetheless exhibiting an astonishing lack of understanding, implying that Mr. Wells is among the lowliest of artists. Mr. Wells can afford to do without such admirers!

Who do you think you are, anyway? You seem to compare Mr. Wells with a politician; it is the politician's profession to invent facts. And who has given you the right to call his scientific treatment a "novel"? You write that he has imagination. Do you dare to compare him to his cook? His cook has imagination, as do all untrained minds. Mr. G.B. Shaw—who is also much admired by Germans— has also had the pitiful audacity to call Mr. Wells a novelist; he doesn't seem to realize that he himself is an incurable fantasist and distributor of lies, who has smuggled a new ideology into our literature under the deceiving package of "realism." But then, maybe he does realize this, for it reflects his level of intelligence, as well as his potential dangerousness!

But no matter who is what: Mr. Wells informs you that all poets can go to the Devil! Poetry is something for children and primates, and even children should be saved from this poison by an intelligent and practical education. Poetry leads to the loss of precision, to lazy thinking and even to immorality. Someone who systematically gets into the habit of drifting away from the truth, yes, someone who even goes so far as to take pride in his bold slurs over reality, will soon lose his precision concerning other matters of life too.

*Wer Lügt, der stiehlt** is one of your proverbs, and a short survey of reality shows us that in practice all poets are indeed thieves. Your own German classics were modeled after our Shakespeare, and he himself was the king of thieves. However even when poets take the trouble to write down their own thoughts, they turn out to be a cheap affair after all. Because it is a hundred times easier to invent something than to discover something, and it is a hundred times simpler to work a fantasy out in

---

*Translator's note: Meaning "A liar is also a thief," old German saying.

detail than to really search into facts. That is why Mr. Wells sympathizes with Plato, who had forbidden the lecture of Homer, and also with our great philosopher Mr. Hume, who said: "All books which don't contain the facts about experiments, or numbers, sizes and weights, belong in the fire!" Mr. Wells finds the dry but solid excavation reports of Schliemann incomparably more suspense-filled than the tempestuous but unfounded drivel of the *Iliad,* and he thinks a logarithmic table decidedly more original than the whole of Dante's *Divine Comedy.*

From all of this, I think it will be possible for you to deduce which of the two "possibilities" mentioned in your letter is the correct one. From those two, the second one, suggesting that Mr. Wells' work is a free invention of the mind, is absolutely *no* possibility, because a scientifically truthful reporter who invents something cannot exist. Possibly such illogical people are to be found in your own environs, but not among us. The structure on which you support your presumptions shows only too clearly your own complete ignorance. The doubting words of the Time Traveler are of course to be interpreted as ironic remarks, something which should be clear even to the most simpleminded reader!

As for what concerns Mr. Blank, he isn't described as the "most intelligent and serious-minded" of the group of listeners around the Time Traveler; on the contrary, he is shown as being the most narrow-minded and superficially intelligent of the circle, and this also should be obvious! His profession itself is proof of that. Haven't you digested the fact that he is a newspaper publisher? Furthermore, one of the biggest! But no, you hardly seem able to read anything between the lines and draw correct conclusions from what you've read. Again, this too is an understatement! Your third chief witness for the prosecution, the journalist Mr. Anthony Transic, is silent during the whole evening, out of absolute stupidity, and surely not because his silence is meant to convey anything to the reader.

The other "possibility" stated in your letter makes absolutely no sense either, in the way you choose to put it. The report of the Time Traveler does not contain some "grains of truth," it is the whole truth, containing not a single grain of fiction. Surely, in your country people must have strange notions about the respectability of a writer! In all seriousness, do you imagine it possible for a respectable author such as Mr. Wells to have the audacity, the impudence, to add something to the report of a scientific experiment of the highest importance, or even take something out of it? Do you perhaps think that a brilliant scientist such as Mr.— has made his dangerous experiment exclusively to give Mr. Wells the ideas for a few novelistic fantasy games?

Your speculations about the possibility of the real existence of the Time Traveler as weighed against the possibilty of his nonexistence would be laughable if they were not so offensive. First, your belief in his existence as only a literary figure is typical of a certain type of continental insolence and suspicion. Then, when you condescend to posit the Time Traveler's existence—which of course is a fact—you again commit an unforgivable indiscretion: only if he were a creation of the mind would you have had the right to inquire about what happened to him afterward. Thirdly—and finally—it is complete arrogance on your part to write to Mr. Wells telling him what he should and what he shouldn't do. Precisely because he realizes his obligation to the Time Traveler and to his own reputation, he must refuse you any explanation. You can compare the pro-

priety of his refusal with the indelicacy of your
request.

> Sincerely,
> Dorothy Hamilton,
> Secretary.

P.S. Your request for an autograph is also rejected by Mr. Wells. As he is a writer by profession,
he only does write professionally, and hasn't the
slightest inclination to deliver some of these writings
to private persons. He feels your request to him
insensitively impudent. Would you ask an account-
ant, whose profession is counting, to add a column
of ciphers (and preferably a very long one) for
your own private enjoyment? You as an actor surely would be very surprised if one of your "admirers"
would have the boldness to ask you to memorize a
difficult role in a play just for his own pleasure.

3

To Mr. Anthony Transic, London.

Vienna, February 19th, 1908.

Dear Sir!
The enclosed copies will inform you about my
correspondence with Mr. Wells. I am grateful to Mr.
Wells, for it was in his letter that I obtained your
name, which is not mentioned—I couldn't say if
deliberately, or carelessly left out—in the novel,
or rather the *report* on the Time Machine.
I am absolutely certain that this letter, though it
lacks a more complete address, will reach you without any signficant delay, because the London postal

office is so resourceful and efficient that it even managed to deliver a letter without a specific name and address, namely to the Time Traveler. Although it could be said, *did not deliver*. To explain this seeming paradox, I'll relate the following:

Immediately after having received Miss Hamilton's letter, I dispatched a telegram to "The Time Traveler, London," and it was promptly returned with the words "Gone on a Journey" marked on it. Now it shouldn't surprise anyone that a traveler had gone on a journey, but I really would have liked to learn *what kind* of a journey. Is he *still* traveling in Time? Or, *again?* Or for a change has he gone on a very ordinary journey, as all mortals do? However, the postal office isn't in the habit of passing on such detailed information. Nevertheless, this exchange has proven without the shadow of a doubt that indeed the Time Traveler does exist.

I do not want to admit that I was still in doubt myself about this, after what Mr. Wells, or rather his secretary, wrote to me. I have always considered Mr. Wells a very honorable person, and all of this has only put more strength in my conviction. I admit, however, that I now have less respect for his talent, after the disclosures of his secretary. If he has only written a conscientious report on an event which actually occurred, as his secretary admitted, then his literary craftmanship is sadly lacking. Of course the horizon of human knowledge has been broadened, but this is to the Time Traveler's credit, not to Mr. Wells'.

With this revelation in mind, it is clear that Mr. Wells hasn't the slightest right to look down on George Bernard Shaw from the heights of his ivory tower.

Even if we admit that Shaw smuggled ideology into literature, the glory of the package is still his.

There is more of an incentive to swallow a foul-tasting medicine if it is encased in a beautifully presented sweet. Call it weak indulgence perhaps, but the results prove the attractive trappings work. Now that which Mr. Wells so bluntly calls Shaw's ideology contains a treasury of truths too, but they are moral and not physical.

Mr. Wells was on the wrong track if he felt insulted by my mistaken assumption that he is a poet. An insult requires a malicious intent to harm, which in this case very clearly did not exist. So all that I have written surely shouldn't have hurt his dignity.

Now, the philosophy of "pragmatism," founded by the American William James, states the following: "Our complete *Weltbild*, our way of looking at the world, is a convention, a conformity which has been generally accepted because it is a practical one, almost a 'practical fiction'"; and the great French mathematician Henri Poincaré says in his book *La Valeur de la Science (The Value of Science)* that the field of mathematics is also a convention, whether true or false, but still a serviceable one. We have accepted Euclidean geometry, not because it is more exact, but because it serves us better than non-Euclidean. So if lines, planes and cubes are indeed fictions, surely Mr. Wells has no right to feel his scientific honor wronged because I assumed him to write a few fictions.

When Mr. Wells claimed that I compared him with his cook by praising his imagination, he was mistaken; his cook has precisely the required imagination of a cook, and he has the imagination of a Wells . . . or would have had, if he really had invented the report. On the other hand, one could easily imagine his secretary to be his cook for writing such a reply to a correspondent whose only fault is the possession of an enormous interest in the writings of Mr. Wells. I would not like to know what words she does use when she is not restraining herself, as she never failed to mention!

This brings me to the reason behind this letter. Miss Hamilton's answer seems suspicious to me in many ways. If I received a letter about which I thought what Mr. Wells apparently thinks about mine, I wouldn't answer it at all, or at most with a few cold lines. This letter, however, is rather long, much longer in fact than my inquiry, and I can only conclude from this that for some reason or other Mr. Wells has a bad conscience. He himself —through Miss Hamilton, of course—gives a hint of this when he writes near the end of his letter that he feels it his duty to the scientific honor of the Time Traveler to refuse any explanations. Proof of this theory is the strikingly irritated style of Miss Hamilton's letter, an irritation without any real motivation. There is something hidden behind this story, and I would like to find out what it is.

First, I thought the Time Traveler existed because he was known at the postal office. And yet he does not exist, because no one knows where he is and *if* he is. "Gone on a Journey" in the case of this traveler may very well mean a journey into infinity or, which comes to the same, a journey into worlds that are barred to us by invincible spaces of Time. However, I do not believe that he is still on the journey he began in 1905 without having returned even once, for the following reasons. If this would have been the case, Mr. Wells would only have needed to say: nothing new has happened, the Time Traveler is still away. There wouldn't have been any need to deny explanations.

On the other hand, just think about the following problem—I have been puzzling my head off about it. Is it logical that the Time Traveler would return only after *years?* Either he'd return immediately, or he wouldn't return at all. Because even if he stayed half a century in the past or in the future, his Time Machine would give him the ability to arrive exactly at the same moment he left. To spectators here he wouldn't have been away at all, or at most only during the unimportant time-lag which his machine would need to pass through the needed time-planes. As you see, this problem is getting rather complicated; one would almost be tempted to say—mysterious! As mysterious in fact as the behavior of Mr. Wells.

I can hardly write again to Mr. Wells, and I suppose it would be completely useless anyway. Thus, the only ones left are the other friends of the Time Traveler, from which the most probable would have been Mr. Blank, the publisher. I have decided to contact you, however, precisely because you didn't speak a single word during that evening. Experience has shown me that such silent people are usually great letter writers, and besides, you are a newspaperman, and when a journalist knows something, he hardly ever wants to keep it to himself. So, if you really know something of importance concerning the Time Machine, please be so kind as to share your knowledge with me. As for all my other remarks, well, you may think of them as continental prejudices.

Yours sincerely,
Egon Friedell.

4

To Mr. Egon Friedell, Vienna.

London, March 20, 1908.

Dear Sir,

Your letter has been read with the greatest attention, and it was indeed full of prejudices. Especially when it comes to the veracity of an author, they really do seem to have strange ideas in Germany. The monstrous examples you used to rationalize the permissiveness of lies were also badly chosen. Even his own kinfolk, the ancient Greeks, didn't take Homer seriously. Not only Plato, but Heraclitus too called him a harmful man and an unforgivable mythmaker. Pythagoras told his pupils that Homer would have to atone for the fabulous lies he so freely distributed in the caverns of the Underworld. But he was dealt with most accurately and finished off by the philosopher Xenophanes, who stated that if the creator of the *Iliad* would have been born a bull, he would have painted all the Olympians as bulls. But I suppose that all these things are described as *Idealismus* and put aside in your schools in Germany.

I won't deny that there is something really fantastic about the Time Machine, but it is precisely this quality that should prove its reality, I might say. Reality in itself is much more fantastic and has much more imaginative power than all the literary creations of poets. To give an example: poets have never succeeded in creating an imaginary animal which is at the same time original and convincing.

When we look at nature, however, we discover new living things every day; beings which have lived in prehuman times as well as still existing creatures, created without human effort and yet absolutely fantastic: telescopic fishes, wheeled animalcules, starfishes, seals, flying foxes, iguanas, terrible dinosaurs! A single little flower is a product of more creative power than a thousand artistic minds could engender. In fact, the fabulous dragon isn't man's invention, but a memory stolen from the age of the flying reptiles.

I hesitated for a long time before replying to your letter, but finally convinced myself that your keen interest gives you the right to know the whole truth. I would like to point out, however, that I hold no such high respect for curiosity as you seem to. One of the most typical cases in world history, the indiscretion of Columbus, who poked around in the Atlantic Ocean long enough to finally discover America, turned out to be an expensive lesson in the long run. Christian science, color segregation, nicotine poisoning, syphilis, trusts: these are some of the leading contributions this continent has brought us, not to forget the American Way of Life. That's enough for me. And I don't eat potatoes.

But to tell the truth, the reasons given above were not really what decided me to answer you after all. The most important motive was my dedication to my friend, the Time Traveler. I believe that Mr. Wells is following a badly chosen course. The sheer rudeness of his rejection is only inclined to create suspicion. At least he shouldn't have asked Miss Hamilton to answer you, because from what I've read this quick-tempered lady is also a wiseacre. She has used the opportunity to dish out quite a few things of which she hasn't really understood half; furthermore she has taken a badly suited approach.

The attack against Mr. Shaw was completely superfluous: is it his fault that he is obliged to write melodramas to stay alive? (See Shakespeare.) Under these circumstances I can easily understand why you felt Mr. Wells's silence concerning the Time Traveler was the hidden admission of his guilt. And to prove that you were wrong there, I will reveal everything I know.

When it comes to the Time Traveler, there can be no talk of guilt, rather of bad luck or maybe of absentmindedness. You will understand that it was in fact impossible to take really *all* factors into consideration. Well, let's say, until now you couldn't understand everything. But the whole case is actually very simple—as simple as only the absolute truth can be.

The enclosed report has an advantage in that it is composed almost entirely of notes that were written down immediately after it all happened. The immediacy of this report proves its truthfulness. Where the Time Traveler speaks, I have done my best to reproduce his words as correctly and completely as possible. I think I have succeeded there, being the possessor of a very clear memory. Besides, when it comes to reproducing on-the-spot accounts, as an interviewer specializing in face-to-face meetings with personalities, I have a few years experience to rely on. Otherwise I have neither the talent nor the ambition to be a storyteller, but as you will see the Time Traveler himself is not a good story teller either. Prominent scientists seldom are. Newton did write well-known voluminous theological reports, but his use of the storytelling art as displayed in these surely wouldn't have founded his worldwide reputation.

As far as I know there exist only two world famous scientists who at the same time are also great writers: the French Buffon and the German Professor Helmboltz. But there is an explanation for the existence of these two exceptions: Buffon's specialty was the description of natural science, which has not without reason been called natural history. The real mastery of the natural sciences requires an accomplished storyteller. As for Mr. Helmholtz, his specialized field was theory itself. We do honor him for a few admirable inventions, like his *Augenspiegel,** but in reality we must consider him to be a speculative physician; I would almost be tempted to say, a philosopher!

A philosopher creates, in contrast to an investigator who—especially if he is a practical researcher—determines facts. Now the Time Traveler is so absolutely practical, that he is nothing else: he is only interested in the *use* of something, never in the theory of it. He intuitively understands so much of the natural sciences that I'm not sure if he would be able to see the differences between a lime-tree and an oak, and I really couldn't say if he classifies a wolf among the canines or the felines!

From the miserable English of your two letters, I concluded that you haven't mastered this language very well, so I have had the report translated by my wife Laura, whose maiden name is Müller, she being of German birth. As you will appreciate I must ask you to treat these revelations as being of a strictly confidential nature, not to be mentioned to anyone else and certainly not to be made public. After all, some parts of this report do contain material which might be found to be compromising. I hope you now understand that I'm not as stupid as Mr. Wells would have liked you to believe. I didn't open my mouth during that whole evening, not because I'm

---

*Translator's note: Eye mirror.

stupid or because I wanted to convey more with my silence than with words; I kept silent simply because no one asked me anything. We English prefer to speak only when spoken to.

You have asked: here is the answer.

Anthony Transic.

To Refresh One's Memory:
A Short Lesson for the Ignorant and
for Those Who Think They Know
Better.

Before we start with Mr. Transic's account, we will include a short piece here, which is really superfluous for normally intelligent people. This article is directed toward two groups of people: those who are completely ignorant, and that special breed of super-intelligent mule who tries to demolish everything with banal skepticism. You know those types: people like Monsieur Pérès who wrote a thick book in which he tried to prove that Napoleon never really lived but was a personification of the sun; and those Bacon fanatics whose most radical members claim that not only Shakespeare but Cervantes too were pseudonyms used by Bacon.

Up until now, time after time, skeptics have expressed doubts about the actual existence of the Time Machine, some doubting whether it is a possibility at all. These doubts are either the result of that kind of jealous grudge all great inventors have met in their own times, or the complete lack of knowledge of physics. Now that the theory of relativity has been proven, no one should have any reason left to raise objections. The Time Traveler, while explaining the function of his machine, said about the following:

"You know of course that a mathematical line, a line of thickness *nil,* has no real existence. Neither has a mathematical plane. These things are mere abstractions. Nor, having only length, breadth and thickness, can a cube have a real existence. So most people think. But wait a moment. Can an *instantaneous* cube exist? Can a cube that does not last for any time at all have a real existence? Clearly, any real body must have extension in four directions: length, breadth, thickness, and . . . duration! Scientific people know very well that Time is only a kind of Space. Here is a popular scientific diagram, a weather record. This line I trace with my finger shows the movement of the barometer. Yesterday it was so high, last night it fell, then this morning it rose again, and gently upward to here. Surely the mercury did not trace this line in any of the dimensions of Space generally recognized. But certainly it traced such a line, and that line, therefore, we must conclude was along the Time Dimension."

It is impossible to express it more accurately. If I want to estimate the place of an object, I need three datums: how far is it before or behind me, how far to the left or to the right side, and how far is it above or below me . . . and then I still don't know where it is, because I still don't know *when* it is. If I have a rendezvous with a pretty young lady at eighth o'clock, and we agree we'll meet again two days later, same time, same place: the fourth bush to the left of the park's gates . . . well, it won't be the same place, because the Earth will have moved, the sun will have changed position, and with it the whole planetary system.

The sun is moving toward the fixed star Vega at

a rate of twenty kilometers each second. "Fixed star" isn't a very truthful definition, because Vega moves with a speed which is a third greater than that of our sun. But this is nothing compared with our galaxy, which is running through the universe at six hundred kilometers a second, a thousand times the velocity of a cannon ball. Will the fourth bush then still be at the same place after two days? For the young lady and me, it will be "the same place" but a serious impartial observer will truthfully admit that the two places are *not* the same, only similar, just as a die of seven meters and another die of seven plus two meters length, breadth and height resemble each other.

The exact definition of the second rendezvous location should be—if we assume that the first took place on May 7th this year—"fourth bush to the left of the gates, on May 9th, eight o'clock in the evening." Please note: the definition of place! Only when possessing these coordinates would a cosmic observer—who hasn't automatically moved with the Earth, the sun, Vega and the whole galaxy— be able to return exactly to the first rendezvous place.

Whoever believes that the time definition is superfluous would be as childish as the passenger on board a transatlantic ship who thinks that he is in the same place when he seats himself on Wednesday in the same easy chair he sat in on Monday. All living beings and all objects are sitting in such an easy chair all the time!

The only exceptions are the ghosts who—as one says—are living in the Fourth Dimension. Which means that they are able to move forward and backward in Time, whereas we can only move in the three directions of Space. This enables them to turn up now and then as revenants out of the past, or even predict the future as spirits contacted by mediums. In this way many objectively recorded messages of dreadful things to come, mysteriously attributed to dead persons, can be explained very naturally. Many things no longer appear as "miracles" to us, if we decide to look at them through the eyes of practical physics.

This also explains the fact that concrete matter is no barrier to ghosts. Matter possesses four dimensions, and we only have the ability to move through three of them. Wrongly, we believe that our barrier is space, exactly that dimension which is open to us on all sides and in all directions! Our greatest barrier is Time, to which we are—if you allow me to put it this way—fastened. If we were plane beings, who could move only in the two dimensions of left and right, or forward and backward, the third dimension of height and depth would be the greatest barrier and mystery to us, the domain of the spirits. So we still consider the unknown Fourth Dimension as the spiritual one.

We can conclude from this that people who still neglect the facts of so-called ghostly phenomena are only kept from accepting the truth by their mental backwardness and doubtful mathematical schooling. The belief that there are only three dimensions is a primitive superstition; doubting the existence of the Fourth Dimension is the skepticism of a schoolboy first learning his three R's. Wireless communication has for a long time been thought of as something absolutely unscientific, impossible, even by the great Newton. Nowadays even the most unskilled, untutored farmhand possessing a radio just takes its existence for granted. Not even fifty years ago, the great Billroth refused to be present at an experiment with hypnosis; in our day the law brings action against the unqualified use of hypnosis, surely the greatest official recognition possible!

In the same way Kant—surely the greatest mind this world ever saw—in his satirical *Traume eines Geistersehers (Dreams of a Ghost Seer)* put Swedenborg down as a fanatic and an unbelievable fantast, though his telepathic achievements had been scientifically proven.

All these phenomena—wireless communication, hypnosis, telepathy, spiritism—even today have been called "absolute nonsense." But it is in such "absolute nonsense" and in nothing else that the progress of human knowledge is contained.

The remark of the Time Traveler that Time is only another dimension of Space was a genial anticipation of the theory of relativity. It has been undeniably concluded that each place has a certain time, that time is an essential function of each place. Therefore we can use for Time as well as for Space a common measure: this unit is the "time-meter," meaning the time which light needs to cover the distance of one meter. Light, as you know, has a velocity of three hundred thousand kilometers per second, from which follows that for one kilometer it needs a three hundred thousandth part of a second, and for one meter a thousandth part of *that:* a three hundred millionth part of a second. This is the time-meter. It seems to us an incredibly small measure, but this is a relative point of view.

The time-meter is fused with the slowness of our perception possibilities. If this would be nearer the velocity of light, we would be able to perceive that Time moves. But conversely we wouldn't be able to notice the movements of Space and the objects it contains! We may conclude this only as the results of astronomic observations; similarly, we must conclude the movement of Time solely through the results of observations of that type.

To someone possessing a perceptive sense working at lightning's speed, thrown stones wouldn't fall but would appear to float. They would have moved almost no distance from one place to another during a man's lifetime, and oldsters would tell their grandchildren about the history of such stones. The velocity of the mightiest cannon ball would be one meter in about six days, and it would indeed be an astronomical phenomenon! Turned in the other direction, our abilities of perception and understanding need almost ten years to cover one single time-meter, as the year contains about 31½ million seconds. No wonder indeed that we simply can't see such bigness, and prefer to neglect it, as the mathematicians say.

To us objects don't expand in the directions of "before" and "afterward": we still believe that an object at four P.M. is exactly the same at four A.M., just because the other three dimensions haven't changed. But this object is the same only in our limited understanding and knowledge. It is the same mistaken assumption that man made when he believed the Earth was fixed and unmoving, just because it seemed that way to him. We know better about that now but we still believe that Time is fixed and unmoving.

In the routine of daily life these two errors are of no real importance. The sun still rises and sets for us as well as it did for Ptolemaeus. Ironically, there's not a single human being who remembers to say, not the sun, but the Earth rises and goes down. In just this unthinking manner we continue to hold onto the fictional belief that time is fixed, a peaceful womb in whose embrace all objects rest. It is a prejudice, but not a dangerous one. We will still find the pretty young lady at the fourth bush to the left of the gates, and if she isn't on time, she won't blame it on the Fourth Dimension. But in reality we *are* fixed, because we can't move in Time.

We are fixed, but not the Time Traveler. Because —even if he isn't a ghost—he has the opportunity to move up and down the Fourth Dimension, as we do in the third. His invention is based on a very simple principle, so simple that he has found it superfluous to explain it. As a matter of fact, all basic inventions are as simple as the egg of Columbus. Just look at the windlass and the potter's wheel, to give but two examples. Yet without a doubt it took a long time before someone discovered their principles! And is there anything more simple than a dynamo? The electric current magnetizes steel, the magnetism of the steel on the other hand creates an electric current. Werner Siemens caused magnets to be intensified by currents, then the currents were intensified again by the magnets. By this ever changing—and ever mounting—game he finally obtained a strong and constant source of power, which has since then changed the face of the Earth. One would think every schoolboy would have had such an idea.

The Time Traveler reasoned like this: usually we move through three dimensions—or think we do. In reality however we only move in *one* dimension: forward or backward, to the left or to the right, up or down. To put it shortly: with each movement we make, we *isolate* one dimension. This may be illustrated clearly using the dimension upward. If I'm climbing a mountain, I do happen to move sideways *and* upward, thus in two dimensions, but this is only because my movement upward isn't complete. A skylark, a jet of water, a balloon—even a small one used as a children's toy—rises up as straight as an arrow.

A primitive man who could only use his feet, or at best be seated on horseback, and move upward this way, didn't think about the way he moved. But with the rise of civilization, man began to make machines which did isolate the direction of movement consciously: elevators, cars, airplanes, even rockets. Think about the pilot of an airplane, and about a deep sea diver: they each in their own ways isolate the dimension of up or down. Think about a man pushing a wheelbarrow: he too isolates the direction at which his nose is pointing.

This is what the Time Traveler does with the Time Dimension: he isolates it. In fact we are doing the same—as I've said before—but we do it unawares because the covered distance is so minuscule, being about one time-meter in ten years. We do it unconsciously just as a savage who is running down a hill, not because he wants to isolate the down-dimension, but because he has to get there. The Time Traveler, compared to us, must feel as Mr. Piccard does compared to that savage.

You've seen it yourself: the idea of the Time Machine is so simple that it is almost disappointing, but the idea isn't yet the realization! For this were needed the fabulous technical knowledge and skills of the Time Traveler. Explaining in detail everything which was needed for the creation of the Time Machine is impossible for me. This would take a separate book in itself, and would also require a certain knowledge of higher and highest mathematics from the reader, something which he probably lacks, and which—I have to admit—I don't possess either.

Maybe now you will say that without an explicit scientific demonstration it won't be possible for you to believe in the Time Machine. I can't say much against that, but I would like to draw your attention to the following. You do believe in Newton's law of gravity, and you do believe in the Copernican system. Now, have you seen the proofs yourself? Out of ten thousand men maybe one will be able to, because this requires an extraordinary knowledge of mathematics and physics, a knowledge and understanding almost as immense as that needed to comprehend the Time Machine itself fully.

I will mention only one thing further. Of all the materials needed to construct the machine radium was the most important. It is well-known that this element possesses the faculty to send out Becquerel rays constantly, and by atomic deterioration creates a gas, the so-called emanation. So this is in a way a kind of perpetual motion, ignoring the laws of the continuance of energy. There also exists a special connection between time-energy and this gaseous energy, which is almost impossible to measure and must be found by deducing its presence. Because it is self-evident that there does exist a time-energy, which . . . but you'll find all of this in more detail in Mr. Transic's report.

Chapter I

The Time Traveler Starts

It was on May 4th, 1905 that the Time Traveler began his journey into the past. I was better and more completely informed about the exact nature of his plans than Mr. Wells, because the evening before I had had a long conversation with the Time Traveler. He hadn't the slightest intention of traveling back to the saurians, though I would have liked to see this. You must know that in my free time I'm a passionate zoologist, and it would have been very satisfying to me to learn if Mr. Huxley's theory (to which I have always strongly objected) that the sea animals had been the first, could be disproved this way. I myself put forward the thesis that from the very start there existed animal life on land as well as in the sea . . . that life on land and in the sea are the two great origins of life on Earth. An example to prove this: in the Jura Period there must have been lobsters as well as spiders.

But the Time Traveler had become a bit distrustful and was more careful after the misadventures of his journey into the future. He indicated the great dangers of such an experiment. First of all, he couldn't foresee if he might perhaps arrive in the middle of a Glacial Age, and freeze to death as soon as he got there. After all, with our limited knowledge of prehuman times, the separate parts of the Jura can only vaguely be estimated within the limits of two or three thousand years. Suppose the tower room of his laboratory in which the Time Machine stood became a block of ice, with him in the middle of it! (I scarcely need to mention again that the Time Machine only moves in the Time Dimension, not in space, so the place where it stands remains always the same.) Yes, who could guarantee him that land *did* exist there? Who could tell what the environment of Richmond looked like in the Jura? Maybe it was a gulf stream, four hundred meters below the level of the sea. Maybe it was even the center of an active volcano! It was an open question as to which to prefer: drowning, burning or freezing. And finally, but most important of all, the entire spider-lobster question (including the rest of my theory) didn't interest *him* at all.

As I saw that he hadn't the slightest intention of changing his mind, I tried to direct his interest at least toward the first men. The only thing he had to do was search the terrain with his machine in time jumps of perhaps five thousand years, till he found human trails. Certainly this was a question whose answer was important to everyone.

"To everyone," the Time Traveler exclaimed, "but absolutely not to me! Do you really think I have the intention, or even the desire, to start a feud with backward and pigheaded scientists? If what I found suited their own pet theories, they would explain with superior smiles that they knew this all the time; and if it didn't fit, they would reject the facts with the same smiles, declaring it to be the work of a novice in the matter. I view their whole evolution theory as the work of a novice! *Natura non facit saltus!*"

He had developed a strong dislike against all

"unguaranteed times," as he called them. He even objected to the Antiquities. "They would think my machine a Roman war machine," he flared up, "and it would be received with a shower of arrows. Besides, there's nothing less interesting than Old Britain. Wanting to conquer this country was an incomprehensible hobby of Julius Caesar, almost as incomprehensible as his lack of superstition, which cost him his life. But the English Middle Ages also can go to Hell: exclusively games of robbery and theft!

"And at the time of the Reformation, things in England looked even worse: nothing but stupid and ordinary wars for this or that belief or conviction. If you were a devout Catholic who believed in the Pope, they cut off your head for high treason. If you were an honest Protestant who refused to have anything to do with the ceremonies of the Church, they hung you on the gallows for being an iconoclast. If you were a severe Calvinist who rejected the Holy Communion, they burned you at the stake for being an heretic.

"The lauded Renaissance isn't tempting to me either. One only has to remember what happened to Papin and his steamboat! Just imagine if they destroyed my Time Machine too. What a horrible thought, having to spend the rest of my life under a heavy dirty cap of hair, dressed in a sweaty coarse tunic, without a fork, a night shirt, street lights! With as floor-covering a mixture of street dirt and spilled beer. Imagine that I, accustomed to traveling with my Time Machine, would from then on be obliged to ride in a rotten carriage, getting stuck in the mud of the roads every ten minutes; or maybe in the dark and airless cabin of a sailing ship, in continual danger of running aground or being attacked by pirates; or at the least getting scurvy through the exclusive diet of salted meat and dried vegetables!"

"All right, all right!" I exclaimed impatiently. "But in Heaven's name, what did you construct your machine for, if there's not one single age in history which appeals to you?"

"Because I want to get to the year Eighteen-Forty."

"But whatever happened in that year you can find in any old issue of *The Times!* Besides, as far as I know, there was no extraordinary occurrence then!"

"Oh, but there was! In that year Carlyle delivered his six speeches about heroes, hero admiration and the heroic element in history. How often I've wished to actually hear the warm and sure prophetic sound of that voice, the rich Scottish accent almost like music, that very special fiery flood of words, almost like a descending whirling stream! There were no gramophones in that time, so I'll have to use my Time Machine."

I felt as if struck by lightning. Was this the reason the Time Traveler had created his wondrous machine, using his ingenious mind and abilities? To listen to the heated tirades of a baroque country orator? But at the same time I had to smile about my stupefaction. I knew the Time Traveler was a much too daring and curious researcher to stop there. I knew that, once there, he would have to persevere to the utmost limit of what he could discover. How absolutely wrong I was! I mean, not about him: he certainly didn't lack courage or the drive for exploration. No, I was wrong in my estimate of his discoveries, which certainly turned out to be amazing, but not as fruitful as I had thought they would be.

But it was already late. "When do you start?" I asked.

"Tomorrow morning, punctually at ten A.M."

"Well, I'll be expecting you back a bit after ten in your laboratory then, to learn if Mr. Carlyle really did have such a penetrating Scottish accent. Maybe you'll take a few nice pictures at the same time. Though I do believe they already had a kind of photography or lantern-viewing in his time." I turned to the door.

"No, you'd better not," the Time Traveler called back to me "Please don't expect me back at the time I left!"

"But when *should* I expect you back, and why?" I asked, surprised.

"Well, you see," he replied, a bit confused, "maybe it's only a whim of mine, but I wouldn't like walking around as a prematurely old man."

"What do you mean by that?"

"Well, just suppose that I like the cozy London of the Eighteen-Forties so much that I decide to linger there for half a year, or maybe even longer—three, four, five years. Now, think about it. If I return at the same instant I left, all the people I know wouldn't have changed at all. But I would be older; I would have gotten a few gray hairs, a few new wrinkles on my face, and especially my mind would be older. There would arise a completely inexplicable and paradoxical relationship with my fellow men. Speaking to a friend from my youth, I suddenly would have to say, 'young friend,' and he would think to himself, 'Well, I preserved my looks better than he did!' Someone who was five years younger than I would suddenly be twice as much younger. To clarify my feelings, I would feel like someone who had failed his examinations, and must stay another year in the same class. But even with much shorter time-distances, even with ten or twenty days, something would feel psychically wrong. Time is a very fragile thing and should only be touched subtly. I would almost be tempted to say: with tact and care. For a good reason the German word *Takt*—which we translate as 'tact'—is also used for the time-measure of the rhythm of music. So I will stay away exactly as long . . . as I *did* stay away."

"And how will I know of your return?"

"I will inform you of my arrival immediately, by the same means as we have used till now. All right with you?"

"Good. Thank you. And have a good journey!'

Chapter II

The Mysterious Telegram

After his last disclosures, I didn't expect the Time Traveler back very soon. The deliverance of those few speeches soon would be over, and I strongly doubted that he would feel attracted to Victorian London. Although they didn't use wigs, and their floors weren't covered with dirt and spilled beer, and they did have forks, night shirts, gas lights, matches, steel springs for their beds and the first steamer, I felt sure these comforts wouldn't satisfy the enterprising spirit of the Time Traveler.

So, as I said, I felt certain that very soon he would start on a completely different adventure. When one possesses a fairy tale machine, compared to which Faust's magic cloak was a trifle, and even the most advanced airship negligible, surely one would search for the answers to other questions— was Mohammed a quack? was Cromwell a hero? Therefore I expected him to be away at least for many weeks. I spent the time without feeling any special suspense. However, very soon after he sent me his first message, not in person, but in another and very strange way.

The Time Traveler and I are among the very few private persons in London whose houses have been equipped with stations for wireless telegraphy;

most probably we both are the only ones. Officially almost nothing has been done for the exploitation and perfection of this new invention, so the precursors and those eager to learn must do this on their own initiative.

Any iron balcony or rain-pipe can be used as an antenna, and to receive close emissions these ersatz-antennas are aptly suited. The laying of an emission cable which is long enough is not much more expensive than the construction of a lightning-rod; and with a bit of manual skill one can easily construct a transmitter at home. But strangely enough most people only do sensible things if they are ordered to. They go freely to the American bar by themselves. In any case we reap the profits of this laziness of London's inhabitants: we almost never have any faults during our transmissions. Except for us, the only other Englishmen who communicate by wireless telegraphy are a few ship captains and officials on shore-stations.

We used our telegraphs quite often; most often the Time Traveler was the sender, and I the receiver of his messages. He would telegraph interesting observations to me, the reports on some of his experiments, calculations and sometimes even effectively striking puns or jokes he thought very good. This time too, he had promised me with his last words that he'd let me know of his arrival by the telegraph.

About thirty-six hours had passed since his departure, and it was near ten P.M. when I heard the signal of the telegraph station. I ran to it, and received a telegram from the Time Traveler which struck me with astonishment and confusion. It said:

HORRIBLE UNFORESEEN ACCIDENT.
I'M ALIVE AND WELL, BUT YOU'LL
NEVER SEE ME AGAIN. YOUR HEART-
STRICKEN M.

I couldn't have been more amazed if someone
had hit me on the head with a hammer. In those
first moments I thought it to be a puzzling joke.
But who could be behind it? Only a few of my closest friends knew of the existence of our two wireless
stations; none of the Time Traveler's friends knew
of it: not even Mr. Wells. And I couldn't imagine
one of those few people playing such a tasteless and
crude prank on me. Besides, to fulfill such a bad
joke, the rascal had to have been able to enter the
locked house of the Time Traveler, and surely none
of the gentlemen I knew was capable of house-
breaking.

Slowly I began to get my thoughts into thinking
order. From which point of the Earth did this telegram arrive? In whatever faraway place was the
Time Traveler, so that he had been obliged to use
this means of communication? But this was pure
nonsense! My friend was after all traveling in the
Time Dimension, and hadn't even left the tower
room of his laboratory. Why had he had to use the
wireless station to send me his message, when he
could have taken a coach to reach my house?

Was something stopping him from leaving his
house, so that he had to use this method of communication? Maybe he was sick and in bed. But
no, he had clearly telegraphed: "I'm alive and well."
Or maybe he was in the grip of some enemy power.
But then surely he would have asked for my help!
And what was the meaning of those mysterious
words "But you'll never see me again"? Had he

gone out of his mind? Maybe his daring exploration had driven him so far in Time that he had journeyed into those mysterious boundless depths that touched on infinity. This could easily have traumatized his mind, which was human after all, so that he had returned to the present insane. Which one of all these suppositions was the correct one? Maybe none at all!

I had to know, and I decided that there was only one way to find out: to go to his house immediately. In a terrible hurry, without even bothering to take my hat, I ran to the street. According to the *Guide to London City* there are eleven thousand hackney-coaches in London, and of these seven thousand are hansoms*, but I have never managed to find one when I urgently needed one. I had to take a cab which came aimlessly along. I promised the driver half a pound if he hurried, and so we raced on . . . if I may use that expression!

My friend's mansion gave the impression of being completely uninhabited. Everything seemed quiet and peaceful, bathing in the soft warmth of the beautiful spring night. Crickets were chirping in the distance, and maybugs were joyfully dancing around the gas lights. Buttercups flowered along the garden railings, and from a neighboring mansion the sounds of a gramophone reached me, as it played the chorus of the beautiful song "The Honey and the Bee." Involuntarily I thought that maybe the Time Traveler had arrived at a time when there were no gramophones. On the front door there was a piece of paper: *Gone on a Journey*.

I hammered the knocker against the door; nothing moved inside the house. I began pushing with all the power I had, till the door finally moved. If at that moment a policeman had strolled along, he

---

*Translator's note: The taxis of that era, small two-wheeled carriages.

probably would have thought the worst of a hatless man pushing against the closed door of an empty house.

Of course I had forgotten to bring some matches. I moved blindly through the house, until after a long search I managed to discover a box of matches in his writing-room. The gas supply had been cut off, however, and I had to return first to the gas meter, but finally I succeeded in getting light.

Nothing seemed to have been moved on his writing-desk. In the middle was a table of calculations, which hadn't been there before. Probably he had been working on it shortly before his departure. Next I climbed to the second floor, where his laboratory was situated. Fortunately a forgotten red bulb was burning, almost like an Eternal Light. Again I found the traces of recent work being done here, but nowhere were any essential changes to be found. The Time Machine was not in the tower rooms: so he really had gone on a Time journey!

Was it barely an hour ago that he had sent me a telegram from this place? Absolutely inexplicable!

I left his mansion—the music of the gramophone had in the meantime changed into an ordinary cake-walk—and slowly returned to my own house, my head filled with frightened and confused thoughts.

Chapter III

One Learns the Name of the Time Traveler

I spent the next days and nights fruitlessly puzzling my mind. I took the most adventurous and weird possibilities into consideration. Maybe this was really a ghostly telegram? There are many recorded case histories of *Poltergeister* (mischievous ghosts) which are capable of all kinds of stupidities and monkeyshines. Or maybe he himself was already among those on the Other Side? But no, he had definitely stated "alive," and even supposing that he hadn't meant it literally, and that what he had wanted to state was the higher life in the beyond, even then it wouldn't have made any sense anyway. There's no sense in a ghost describing himself as "alive and well." But then again I had to take in to account that many of the messages that reach us from the beyond through spiritist mediums are often confused, contradictory and unintelligible.

Five days passed in this tortuous brain-picking way. My wife and I were having breakfast and we were still discussing the telegram. My wife had a new pet theory which she was explaining to me. She interpreted the words "You'll never see me again" as a way of putting an abrupt stop to our relationship. She supposed I had hurt the Time Traveler's feelings or angered him in some way or other, and that now he didn't want anything to do with me anymore.

"But he did transmit something about a horrible unforeseen accident," I contradicted her excitedly.

"Well, that accident must have been your behavior," Laura said. "You . . ." and at that moment I heard the signal of the telegraph.

I nearly jumped straight into the apparatus, and read the telegram. "Thank God!" I exclaimed joyously. "He's coming!"

"Who says that?" Laura answered, as she listened with me.

"Well, he telegraphed: 'Be sure to come to my writing-room today at ten minutes to eleven. Else all is lost.' "

"Yes, *you* should go," Laura repeated stubbornly. "but there's nothing in the telegram about himself!"

"But why else would he ask me to come to his house, if he isn't there himself? Besides, why else would all be lost?"

"Well, you'll know it within two hours."

To be on the safe side, I was in his writing-room at half past nine—this time, when I was not in a hurry, not one but two hansoms stood ready, offering their services—and was waiting, full of restrained suspense, for anything which might happen. Not withstanding Laura's objections, I felt absolutely certain that the Time Traveler would arrive with his machine at the announced hour.

Nothing else had changed in his mansion in the meantime, although on his writing-desk I found the picture of a pretty young lady wearing a Stuart collar, which I must have missed the last time. On the backside of the picture were written the words:

They sail along far coasts, but not in their own soul.
(Lactantius) Otherwise unimportant.

At a quarter to eleven, I suddenly heard a buzzing sound on the desk. A misty Something appeared, rotating at an insane speed, which made some papers flow from the desk. It slowed down, became more apparent and finally stood still with a loud knocking noise. I took it in my hand: it was the little Time Machine.

You will remember that the Time Traveler, before he began the construction of the great Time Machine for his own use, had built a small-scale model of the machine, which could travel through Time on its own. Or rather, he had built two: the first he sent—in the presence of several people, among whom myself—as a test into a nonreturnable journey in Time (he didn't know himself if it was into the past or the future); the second one he kept for himself. Apparently it was this one which I had in my hand now. I opened the little machine, and found a sheet of paper. I unfolded it. It was a letter from the Time Traveler, in his own handwriting. I knew those wayward and twisting scientist letters too well. So he was still alive after all, and seemingly of clear mind.

However, as it turned out, the letter didn't tell me much about his current situation. It contained only a few words, written in an extreme hurry; and—being a bit of a graphologist—I could tell from the nervous and feverish nature of the characters that the writer at that precise moment had been in a situation of very extreme psychical or physical strain. At some places an "is" or "and" had been carelessly left out. Without any doubt the letter had been written in a hurry or in confusion. It read as follows:

Dear Mr. Transic. Please go to the second bookcase to the left of the door; there on the fourth shelf you'll find a number of years of the quarterly "Mind." On the front page of the ninth volume, you'll find a table of ciphers, written with a lead pencil. Tear it out and put it in this Time Machine. Address the whole to December 6, 1904. I beg of you to execute this precisely and immediately. The whole happiness of my life depends on it. From now on I will stay in postal connection with you, in this way.

Though the contents of the letter hadn't made me any wiser, I immediately did what he asked me, and dispatched the Time Machine to the requested day. The operation of the machine is extremely simple. One only has to set the pointer at the wanted time and push down one of the two little white handles, marked *Back*. A droning noise, a circling movement which became more ghostly each second, and then the little machine disappeared.

But what was the meaning of all this? Now I knew the time-place where the Time Traveler was, but what in Heaven's name was he doing in December 1904? Even more confused than the last time—the gramophone was singing: "Oh, please, tell me quick, are you the pretty chick, which yesterday night, must've been about eight, laughed at me so right?"—I left the mansion.

Laura said only, "I told you right away that he wouldn't come himself!"

The next day, the telegraph woke me at five A.M. The message contained only five words:

MISERABLE. WHERE IS THE MACHINE?

The following week, a veritable torrent of similar warnings began to arrive at the oddest times of day and night, and in the most disparate moods: threatening, begging, accusing, ordering, demolishing, so that in the end Laura and I began to think we were being driven mad.

Why hadn't the little Time Machine arrived? I had addressed it carefully; I was absolutely sure that I hadn't made any mistake. But we especially despaired because we were unable to find out from where the telegrams came. To discover this, I spent a whole day in the Time Traveler's house while I ordered my wife to note the exact time when the telegrams arrived. That day four telegrams arrived, but no one touched the Time Traveler's sender.

Eventually the telegrams became scarcer, until they finally stopped. The last one said:

YOU ARE A RHINOCEROS!

After that time weeks and weeks silently passed. We still spoke for hours about our missing friend, but we had no hope left. I often used to walk past his house, but it was now more with a sentiment of pity. When I looked at the lonely mansion, it was with sadness. In there he had disclosed so many daring and original ideas, which now were only powerless dreams because the only one who could have turned them into reality had gone on a dark journey.

One evening—it was the sixth of July—I was again standing in his garden, brooding about the imperfection of human knowledge. It was a beautiful evening, just like the time I had received the first telegram. Again night moths were dancing around the flame of the street light, along the gate wild roses flowered, frogs were croaking, trying to drown the sound of the gramophone, which was now proclaiming the latest hit: "Yes, such a car, that's all; something special, something small, something tall." It was then, through the lighted window belonging to the Time Traveler's writing room, that I saw a tall, slightly stooped silhouette which waved a tired hand at me.

"Is it really you?" I mumbled dazedly.

"Yes." The tired voice of Mr. James Morton had answered me, because that's who he was.

Chapter IV

The Resistance of Earth-Time

He seemed more than a bit worn out. He was pale, with deep-set eyes, his clothes were neglected and in disorder, his face was thinner and he had a red nose; he had also grown noticeably older, and involuntarily I thought, *Maybe he really has been away much longer than two months.*

He asked me to sit down, and then said with a rough voice: "I've been back for a few days. But I haven't yet come to my senses completely. I've had quite a few adventures. But fortunately it's all over now. The main thing—the Time Machine is a mistake. It's absolutely impossible to use it in the past. But strictly speaking, scientifically, it's not for the future either. Outstripped. A stupid toy."

"But . . ." I began.

"I will explain it all to you. Of course I should have foreseen it all, if I would have taken the trouble to think about it in advance. And so would you. But at least you have the excuse that you're married."

"Yes, but . . ."

"You'll get it all in chronological order. It still tires me a bit."

"Wouldn't you like a glass of port? You look very tired and nervous."

The Time Traveler refused violently. "No. No alcohol. I've had enough of that. But a smoke of my pipe will do me a lot of good. You don't object if I mix my tobacco while telling my story?"

He didn't wait for my answer, but immediately began with the greatest diligence and a certain display of pomposity to mix his tobacco. This he did by mixing about a dozen different home-grown and foreign tobaccos in a very precise manner. First he simply put them all together, then he started rubbing and kneading the mess with his two hands. He separated it into small heaps, which he treated a second time in the same way. Finally he poured the whole into a polished wooden box, which he shook thoroughly.

This primitive occupation seemed to relieve and distract him. This time, however, I had the idea that he did it for a completely different reason—to hide a certain embarrassment. Something resigned and uncertain had come over him, something which I had never noticed before: a certain melancholy which seems typical of people who have lived through something humiliating or hurtful. It was a really strange performance as he started his bizarre account in a slow and toneless voice, while at the same time he seemed intensely occupied in mixing his tobacco.

As time passed, however, he began to warm up and, near the end, I think his old cheerfulness took over again, that special merriment which is the power of the real thinker, as it teaches him to overlook the banalities of life.

"Exactly at ten o'clock," he began, "London time of course, as my machine had been adjusted to that, I started my journey as I had planned . . . or rather: I tried to start. I put a message on my front door on behalf of the postal services; being a careful man

I turned off the gas meter, went to the tower room and climbed into my machine. I switched it to moderate velocity, and pushed the handle to *Back;* but nothing happened. I pushed further, and finally I was pushing as far as I could, taking a risk that I would reach a much too high starting velocity which might carry me beyond the year Eighteen-Forty. But nothing moved, the pointer of my chronometer stayed unmoving at zero.

I checked the machine completely in all its separate parts, everything was in working order. I got in again, but the damn thing hadn't changed its mind. I spent the rest of that day looking over all my calculations, but absolutely everything was correct, I had made no mistakes. Something was clear now: I must have missed some special condition, a principal barrier.

"In such cases—because you can imagine that it wasn't the first time that my calculations had been obstructed by something unknown and unforeseen— I usually take a drink on it, while thinking it over. I do not share the ideas of those extreme anti-alcoholics, who believe that alcohol always softens and undermines the power of the human mind. Sometimes it can be of very good service when it comes to the sudden understanding of the relations of completely different matters, or to the sudden discovery of almost absurd new combinations— and many great discoveries and inventions have been made that way!

"So I made myself a good grog, and as it was May already, I chose my famous 'cold grog.' The recipe I used to make this excellent drink is, as you may know, very simple. I take a glass and fill a third of it with ice water, then the rest is Jamaica rum: a very refreshing summer drink. If you want to make it a bit more complicated, you can also add ten grams of sugar to each glass. I do think, however, that this is carrying finesse too far, and, besides, I think the use of sugar is unhealthy. So I was drinking slowly and methodically, staring into space and trying not to think of anything at all. Because the rum spirit always works best if there is nothing to disturb him.

"I can't recall how many glasses I emptied when, as I had expected, there was a lightning solution to the problem. I had quite simply neglected the resistance of Earth-Time. I didn't quite see yet how I could conquer this obstacle, but I was satisfied that I had at least the key to the mystery in my hand. The search for a practical solution would have to wait till the next day anyway, when my mind had a chance to rest a bit. So I went to bed and had a good, long sleep, as one can only have after such an excellent sleeping potion."

Chapter V

The Lady from the Day After Tomorrow

The Time Traveler had at last finished with the precise art of mixing his tobacco, and began filling his long, fine pipe. Slowly he repeated: "The resistance of Earth-Time, you understand?"

"Well . . . not exactly," I answered.

The Time Traveler lit his pipe and began speaking in a faraway, pained voice.

It should be clear, it's so simple. Each object not only *is* time, but also *has* a certain time. In other words, not only does it extend into, or has a time-dimension, but it also possesses a certain time-energy. The time-energy of an object can be expressed in the distance it moves in time-units. Let's take a cannon ball: it moves four to six hundred meters in one second; these four to six hundred meter-seconds are its time-energy. Just as any other form of energy, this can be potential energy (restrained energy) or living energy (active energy) Every thrown stone, fired arrow or water jet possesses a specific time-energy, which we very unscientifically call its "velocity."

You know that Helmholtz has fixed the "mechanical warmth equivalent" as the unity of spacial energy: the quantity of warmth needed to raise the temperature of one liter of water with one degree Celsius, is the equivalent of the mechanical power needed to raise half a kilogram four hundred twenty-five meters. Each chemical, electric, magnetic or spacial power prestation can be calculated along the same lines.

The basic unit of measurement of time-energy—its H.P. in Time, if I may put it this way—is the velocity of light: three hundred thousand kilometers in one second; a really amazing quantum of energy. Most objects on Earth of course possess only a microscopically small part of this energy. If we use the formula of Leibniz, we arrive at the following: the energy equals the product of the volume m and the square of the velocity v. This velocity can be found by dividing the distance s by the time t. So the end formula is:

$$m\left(\frac{s}{t}\right)^2$$

So you see that the cannon ball we were talking about, which seems to possess a very great time-energy, has in reality very little of it, because it is small in volume and the v of it is smaller still, as its numerator s is six hundred meter-seconds, its denominator t on the other hand is three hundred million meter-seconds (the velocity of light) and its square three hundred billion.

My Time Machine seems to be a real breakthrough! Until you realize that at the same time all people possess a certain time-energy, with which they move even without my Time Machine, but not as quickly: with their own Time Machine, the biggest one possible—*the Earth!*

As every child knows, the Earth rotates every twenty-four hours around its own axis: this power accumulation of time-energy we call our "day." Someone in electronics will speak of so-and-so much "volts" when it concerns tension, and of "ohm" when it is about resistance, and in the same way we call the Earth-Time prestation seven "days," thirty "days," three hundred sixty-five "days." We can even calculate the time-energy of one "day" by multiplying the volume of the Earth with the square of its velocity. This velocity $\frac{s}{t}$ is the same as the circumference of the Earth, being forty thousand kilometers, divided by twenty-four hours or 86,400 seconds, which comes to four hundred sixty-three meter-seconds.

The velocity of Earth is less than that of our quickest projectiles, because its volume is too great. When compared to my Time Machine this energy, which we'll call for short "Earth-Time," is not very great. If the earth rotated on its axis in twelve hours, and the circumference was eighty thousand kilometers, the Time Machine on which we are traveling all the time would be four times quicker than it is now; the "Earth-Time" would be four times as big, and one Earth-second four times shorter. You understand this, don't you?

Now let's speak about *my* Time Machine, which can create energies that are considerably greater. But one shouldn't forget one factor: my Time Machine is still a Time Machine of Earth. From this follows that it possesses also the same quantum of Earth-Time as all other objects on this planet. Further away, I can choose each time-place at will with my Time Machine, but not the place where I started: that one is absolutely fixed and unreachable by me, as it will always be the present, indicated on my dials at the point "zero."

Now these two factors were unimportant to me; furthermore, both acted to my advantage as long as I journeyed in the future, meaning *along with* Earth-Time. However, as soon as I wanted to go into the past, thus *backward* or *contrary* to Earth-Time, this energy created a barrier, a resisting wall of Earth-Time that I had to conquer.

You might think that this should be very easy: after all, Earth-Time is very small compared to the quantum of energy my machine can create. Certainly! However, each movement needs a certain starting velocity, no matter how small, an impulse to set it moving. Where should I find that? I couldn't do anything with Earth-energy against me, because as long as my machine was not in movement it remained unchangeably and helplessly stuck in Earth-Time, which is constantly moving forward. So to start I needed precisely that Earth-Time which is the only power that could give me the absolutely necessary starting velocity. That's why my start in the future went so easily.

To sum it up with one phrase: *I couldn't push off*. A really ridiculous situation: my gigantically powerful machine was at war with those stupid four hundred sixty-three meter-seconds of Earth-Time . . . and it lost!

The solution, however, came the next morning, as I was still meditating about the problem in my bed. I only had to journey a bit forward, using the Earth-Time to push off into the future, then stop, turn around and journey backward. Then my machine would have acquired a sufficient quantum of potential time-energy to conquer the resistance of Earth-Time. You see? I had to *fill* my machine with time-energy; it was the only way to jump without difficulties over the "now" and its opposing movement forward. Just as a jumper has to make a running start, I had to do the same with my Time Machine, with the difference that to take a running jump, one goes a few steps backward . . . I'd have to go a few steps forward in Time, in order to jump backward!

I felt so satisfied with this solution that I decided to start immediately. I had had a good sleep, and the weather outside was beautiful: birds were singing loudly in the fresh May morning, the whole of nature seemed to be full of good-smelling life, reaching joyfully toward the sun. I got dressed in a hurry, took my camera and field glasses and started at exactly ten minutes past seven toward May the seventh.

I was in a very good humor. To conquer the barrier of Earth-Time of the "now" of one day of time-energy would have been sufficient; however, to be absolutely certain I took twice the needed quantum. Of course the tower room hadn't changed at all at my arrival. As I began turning around, however, I suddenly remembered that in my hurry I had completely forgotten to take a bath and to have breakfast. So I went downstairs.

In my writing-room, however, I discovered that things had changed a bit after all: the weather had changed to fog and downpouring rain and, secondly, a young lady was sitting there who certainly hadn't been there before. She had a really unique appearance, her hair the color of bronze and eyes as blue as the sea; my guess was that she was a student. Unmovingly she was sitting in the melancholy twilight of the rainy day, looking darkly in front of her.

When I came inside, she nervously jumped up, and exclaimed with surprise: "Now what are *you* doing here?

"Now what are *you* doing here?" I involuntarily repeated, rather impolitely I admit. To correct my attitude, however, I continued: "You must excuse me but, you see, I live here."

"Yes, I know that," the strange lady said, controlling herself, "and *you* must excuse me. If I had guessed that you'd be back so soon, I would never . . . I don't know how to explain this to you . . . you must think it very unfitting of me . . . but I did have the feverish desire to see for once these rooms in which such a man . . . and today as I was passing your house on my way to the university, I noticed that the door wasn't closed and then . . ."

"I'm sorry if I have disturbed you," I said, slightly confused.

"Well, you did disturb me," she said hesitatingly. "You see . . . I wanted to bring you my picture . . . but of course only when you were away. . . . I had imagined that you would have found it sometime when you'd be sitting back at your writing-desk. . . ."

Indeed, lying on top of my writing-desk was her picture. "Well, thanks very much," I said. "The picture is really lovely. But something is written on the back of it . . . a quotation from some preacher, if I'm not wrong. I don't get the point completely. . . ."

"Yes, I know, a pity," she said, and again a dark expression came over her face. "Maybe it would be better if I took it back with me after all," she went on. "This is not the way I'd intended to give it to you."

"Well, why don't you forget that I've been here at all?" I said and, as I felt embarrassment growing in me, I added: "I must be going away in a minute. Would you perhaps want to watch my start?"

"Oh yes, with pleasure," she replied joyfully.

While mounting the stairs I asked, less out of curiosity than to sustain the conversation: "But how in fact did you know about my journey?"

She looked down at her feet. "Well . . . first of all, there was the note on your door, and then . . . but again this wasn't very delicate . . . I did listen to a few of your messages to Mr. Transic. . . ."

"Oh no, you couldn't!" I exclaimed, honestly astounded now. "And I have always thought that Mr. Transic and I were the only two wireless operators! Where did you learn that?"

"I'm studying mathematical physics," she said, reddening.

"And from there your display of interest? If you'd asked me, I would have guessed art history!"

"Yes, from there my interest," the pretty scholar-lady repeated.

I was sitting in the saddle of the machine now. "I'll tell you everything about me," I said.

"You'll tell me about yourself?" she asked attentively.

"Yes, everything, all the adventures during my journey."

"Oh, that! But I'll read that in all the newspapers anyway."

"But I'll tell them to you first."

"I can hardly accept that. I can't take all that valuable time from you."

"But nobody has as much time as I have! I own all the time in the world!"

The strange lady didn't answer immediately. Then she softly said: "So you think. No one owns as little time as you.

"I don't quite understand that."

"Now," she continued vividly, "but you are a traveler. I admit, you are probably the most original traveler this world has ever seen . . . but you are still a traveler! The traveler looks at the world; but the results from this are he never looks at the only world which is absolutely real: his *own* world. That is why world legends have cursed Ahasuerus with the most terrible punishment available as he refused a place of rest to Christ: it made him into an eternal traveler on the face of the Earth. And why do people always travel to far places where in fact they have nothing worth searching for? Because they can't live with themselves! And it is this same feared 'I' from which they try to hide in far countries that travels along with them as an eternal stowaway, an unseen passenger which can never be left behind."

I was moved a bit by her words. "My dear girl," I said, "when you speak this way about the depths of the soul, one would almost tend to forget that you are also beautiful!"

"These are wonderful words," she said, her face turned away, "but they are only words. Now please, start! I beg you to!"

I wanted to say something else, but her look was so pleading, that involuntarily I pushed the handle. But again the machine refused to move! I pushed and pushed, but the same thing happened as had a few days before: the pointer remained fixed at "zero."

The pretty student was looking at my trials with sympathy, and I explained the matter. "Dear God!" I cried desperately. "Is there again something which I haven't thought of?"

"I can't judge that," she said, "but if I may give you one word of advice: just start!"

"But where to?"

"Anywhere. It doesn't matter, as long as it works."

"But that's taking a big risk! I won't always have the good luck to find such an enjoyable companion as this time. What if I get into some dreary time of supercivilization, where people live in giant cities below the surface of the Earth—because I feel pretty sure that it will come to that—or maybe in the barbaric times of a new migration of the nations, and I can't get back!"

"You don't have to fear that. One time or another it will work. After all you did get back safely from your first journey into the future, didn't you?"

"Yes, that's true! This train of thought seems logical. You are intelligent, Miss . . ."

"Gloria. But I'm not so very intelligent at all. Man gets his ideas through his conscious mind, we only by our . . . intuition."

"But you really do take a serious interest in my work?"

"Absolutely. Would I have risked entering here if it wasn't for that?"

I had again mounted the machine. "Miss Gloria," I said, "please listen to me. May I ask you to stay here for a few minutes? I don't know where or when I'll travel to, but I know where I'll return to. I will return here, to the seventh of May. I'll return to *you* here."

She shook her head. "Don't do that, Mr. Morton," she said softly but firmly. "I won't stay here another minute. It wouldn't be of any use. Our times are too different."

"You mean so different that they'll never be able to meet?"

"Yes," she whispered, and then, almost as if she were speaking to herself, she slowly added: "Unless . . ."

"Unless . . . ?" I asked, and bent to her. But her words would remain unfinished, because while mov-

ing in the seat of the machine, I accidentally pushed
the handle toward the strongest velocity, and before
Miss Gloria was able to finish her sentence, I was in
the year Nineteen-Ninety-five.

Chapter VI

London in the Sky . . . Literally

Angrily I stopped. The machine was still in the tower room, which helped a bit to better my humor. After all it was rather complimentary to learn that it still existed after ninety years. As I looked closer, however, I began to notice several changes. The walls were made of a kind of almost fluid metal, which softly showed all the colors of the rainbow. Trembling bars of blue-green light were around the ceiling.

I went outside, but not without taking my machine with me. I had suddenly remembered just in time that it wouldn't be quite healthy to arrive in the tower room in the year 1840, because in that year it hadn't been built yet: I would have arrived in mid-air, and would have fallen down from the height of two floors.

I put the machine against the wall of my house, and looked around. Not the smallest sign of any vegetation: as far as I could see, there was nothing but a monotonous glass-like, softly vibrating plain. No sounds anywhere in the air around me: probably there were no animals left, and also no gramophones! Yes, I would almost say that there was no air left as we knew it: it tasted like nothing, and its flatness reminded me of distilled water.

I raised my field glasses, but no matter how far I looked, I couldn't find a trace of London. As I put the glasses down, I noticed a young man in my vicinity. The expression on his face was intelligent but uninterested. Unmoving, he stood before a snake of black light. He answered my greeting with a downcast flicker of his eyelids, and said: "You are a High-Scot?"

"No, I'm not," I answered, slightly surprised. "What makes you believe I am?"

"Because you are dressed in the ancient national clothes, which are only worn by the peasants in High-Scotland."

I hadn't thought of that at all. Of course I could imagine that my striped suit with its high collar and stiff cuffs looked a bit strange compared to the suit of the man before me, which existed of one yellow asbestos hide, clinging to his body.

I said: "No, there's another reason for this. Surely you must have heard something about a Time Machine?"

"No," the unmoving man replied. "I haven't heard anything of that."

It seemed beneath my dignity to explain it in more detail, and I contented myself by saying: "May I ask you then what exactly you are doing here?"

"I'm an observer for the energy manufactory, Savory & Son."

"And what kinds of energy do you produce there?"

"Which kinds? But there is only *one* existing energy! And of course we produce everything: pelts, eggs, timber, salt, milk, paintings, ore!"

"And for whom do you produce all this?"

"Why, for the people of London!"

"But where *is* London?"

The asbestos man indicated upward with his eyelids. I looked up, and saw a sea of houses with market-halls, recruiting stations, hippodromes, theaters, cathedrals . . . literally in the sky! London wasn't any longer "above the sea" but "above the Earth!" I didn't want to ask the man with the snake of light how this had come to pass, else he surely would have taken me for a Scottish illiterate from out of the mountains. Besides, it was easy to place several factors into the correct combination: clearly one had been able to master the power of gravity, and so change the height of objects at will. I thought: now surely this new situation of London has been the ruin of carrier pigeons, but I suppose the fabulous London fog won't have been lessened with it . . . to the contrary!

Carefully, so as not to exhibit my ignorance too fully, I asked matter-of-factly, "And are people satisfied with the weather?"

"Everybody is satisfied with our weather," the man answered. "You can believe me; why else do you think Savory has been holding the weather-creation monopoly for the whole of South England for four years? Not for nothing has it become a fashionable idiom to say 'As trustworthy as Savory's weather!' Besides, the prices of our clouds are below all competition. But of course, it is impossible to please everyone. When we condensate, they say: with such a rain no one's going to the air-games! And when we sublimate, they complain: on such a beautiful day no one takes a stratocab! No one is ever completely satisfied with everything."

"But, if you'll excuse my saying so, if you produce anything possible, then surely there can't be any needs left?"

"Well yes, that's exactly the great mystery! The more we get, the less we really have! This was already the situation in the forties, when they discovered Ophir*, but on a smaller scale. Did we really get richer out of it? On the contrary! Now it was exactly the same when the custom-houses still were in existence in Europe, with all the separated countries: the more goods one possessed, the poorer one was! You just have to look at me for an example: being an observer, the only thing I have to do is stand here and watch, just in case, contrary to all expectations and knowledge, something goes wrong, exactly like a prompter in a theater. So in fact I don't have anything to do, and as a result my pay is absolutely lousy. And why? Because that bloody energy manufactory with its atomic dissociators and twelve and a half billion horsepower is able to do it all by itself! And to think that for years we were fighting in vain for the twenty-four hour day!"

"Twenty-four hour day? But in Heaven's name, when do you sleep?"

The asbestos man made big eyes. "Sleep? But don't they have ultraviolet where you live?"

"Not . . . everywhere," I stammered, embarrassed.

"Now, I'm afraid you'll have trouble staying with it then, especially now with the surplus labor supply. You see: such as is the situation now of the qualified laborer . . ."

Our talk threatened to pass on to social politics, exactly as the discussions in 1905. I changed the subject by asking: "Is there a place somewhere where I can take a bath and have breakfast? A glass of beer would really be sufficient."

"Beer? What is that? But if you want breakfast, why don't you go up to the city and have an oxygen-snack at the first automatic atomizer you meet? A

---

*Translator's note: Fabulous gold country mentioned in the Old Testament.

bath you can have for free. You just have to turn to the left behind the house and walk into the ultra-red field. Hmph," he added, a bit contemptfully, "you *do* come from far away, don't you?"

"Yes," I finished our dialogue. "I happen to come from a place which is rather far away from here."

I was getting sick of the year 1995, and I don't think I have to explain why. I turned in a hurry toward my machine and stumbled—and fell straight through the asbestos man. He was a projection.

I got into my machine—I had the impression that the seat was wider than I had made it—and pushed the handles. Again the damned things wouldn't work! And this time not only for the past, but for the future too! The sweat of fear appeared on my brows.

It was unimaginable that I'd have to stay here forever, in this horrible year 1995 where they produced paintings in an energy manufactory and where rainbows were a matter of competition! Where they ate oxygen for breakfast and artificial eggs for dinner, and where people bathed fully dressed behind their houses! Where instead of enjoying a good eight hours of sleep in a feather bed, they got radiation treatments with ultraviolet, and where they were provided companionship by talks with fellows who were projected from God knows where!

At that moment, someone pushed a finger in my side, and a nasal voice said: "Mister, what are you doing on my radiodrom?" I would never have thought it possible that I would ever have been immensely grateful for a finger pushed in my side, but now I was!

I had made a mistake: this wasn't my Time Machine. It stood untouched a few steps further away.

A man dressed in a phosphorescent tunic and a helmet of light jumped accurately on top of the other machine, and I heard him mumble: "Whatever got into your mind playing around with my cathode-collector? The worst accidents could have happened. Comedian riffraff! Get yourself a haircut before your first play! Besides, I loathe historical plays!" Immediately afterward he disappeared with a dull report, leaving nothing behind but the hissing ray of a violet-blue flame.

Chapter VII

The Two Egyptians

I mounted my own machine, without spending a further thought on that conceited sports maniac. Now it worked! And not only forward, but also backward! At last I had succeeded in conquering the barrier of Earth-Time. Joyfully I started, at first very slowly, to stay on the safe side.

The sun went down, or rather: it rose in the wrong direction; and it rose, by going down at the wrong point. I changed into a stronger velocity. The moon lost one quarter after another, or rather: it gained them. Gradually vegetation began to appear: cut trees rose on their own power; fruits changed into blossoms; dried leaves turned green; bushes drew in their branches; mushrooms went down into the earth.

Filled with an intense feeling of satisfaction I tasted the air, which seemed to have turned back to normal. One of the many fatal properties of that horrible age from which I had been fortunate enough to escape, was that its air didn't possess any ozone, due to the complete lack of any vegetable life. Savory and other similar forms made it all artificially: potatoes, vegetables, herbs, fruits. Since there existed great Fruit Works, Vegetable Works, and so on, there was no need left for real agricultural plantations. And, of course, with the disappearance of the Earth's vegetation also went all those animals which to our taste charmingly complete a landscape: beetles and butterflies, birds and bees, gnawers and reptiles.

I didn't take the time to find out if the inhabitants of London anno 1995 also created the flesh of animals artifically for their meals. Maybe they had stopped eating flesh altogether. I wouldn't have been surprised to learn that they got drunk on flesh-gases, and invited each other to alcoholic injections!

I was thinking about such sad suppositions, when I suddenly noticed a fearfully threatening change in my Time Machine. Its movements became unstable, it began shaking. The pointers on the dials were moving uneasily back and forth, the machine began losing velocity, it began to move falteringly. A disastrous unknown power was working against the fluid movement of the mechanism of my machine. From where this mysterious power came I couldn't guess, but the results of its interference were only too clear.

In principle, disturbances are of course as likely to turn up in the Fourth Dimension as in the other three, but I had believed that in practice I wouldn't have to take them into account. Maybe the time-energy of the Earth only now began to use its whole power. More probable, however, was that I had arrived in the power field of another Time Machine, and maybe at the end even had had a collision with it! After all, I was now passing 1957, and at that time there might possibly be many Time Machines.

But no matter what the exact nature of the negative power, I had stumbled into a time-shadow and had lost the full control of my vehicle. A rather ticklish situation: imagine an express train moving at full speed, and suddenly losing its driving power.

There was no time to think anything out. Instinctively I acted, doing what I thought to be the only alternative: I turned the machine immediately back, or rather, forward.

I jabbed the forward-handle down, and rushed back: no, forward again into the future with a velocity which made me dizzy, as it was almost one tenth of a time-meter per second. However, I had escaped the dangerous influence field of the mysterious time-shadow just in time.

The pointer showed the year 2123. I exhaled after holding my breath and stopped . . . only to discover that I was floating about twice a man's height above the Earth! The bottom of London had gone down! During the first fragmentary moment of terror, I thought first of my machine rather than myself. But we were already falling.

Fortunately, nothing bad happened as my machine and I sank down in a soft carpet of clay soil. I exhaled for the second time, and looked around at the environment, which had almost been destined to become my eternal resting place. Without any materials or my calculation tables, I would never have been able to reconstruct my machine if it had been destroyed by the fall.

The soil wasn't exactly clay, rather it was a soft but tough mud of a strange yellow-gold color. As far as I could see, the most beautiful growths rose out of it, spreading a spicy, almost drugging scent. There were colossal multileaved violet flowers, cut almost in the shapes of asymmetrical paper kites; giant transparent plants in misty cloudlike colors, which resembled great octopuses set on dry land; and curious bushes bearing two different kinds of fruits: a tall kind of violet-colored banana, and a violent red asparagus, which was meters long.

Nothing moved. Only a great copper-colored

lizard crawled up on me, and seated itself fearlessly on my shoulder. Again, nowhere were any buildings to be seen. I looked up, but London was no longer in the sky.

"So they went underground after all," I said to myself. Immediately thereupon, I spotted two men who were approaching me. Their skins were tanned deep bronze, and their soft beardless features looked festive yet serious. They wore square pieces of wool around their shoulders and loins, else they had no clothing: no shoes, no hats.

When they noticed me, they abruptly stopped; then they made a ceremonial greeting by putting their flattened hands on their foreheads and respectfully walking around me. When they had finished this ritual, the older one spoke to me, using a very pure but ancient English, seemingly out of Chaucer's time. I hadn't heard such language used since my days at high school.

"We are at a loss to explain how the Blessed One arrived here."

I could hardly expect a knowledge and an understanding of my Time Machine from what seemed to be a backward kind of people. So, as best as I could, I tried to explain as simply as possible the essentials of my Time Machine, and what had happened to me so far. They listened very attentively and I could see that they had understood what I had said.

Then the younger one spoke: "Then you must be the Most Blessed One, whom we came here to meet."

"How do you mean?"

"We come from the Sixt Katarakt," the older one answered. "That's where we live and work: the Great School. It has existed for more than three

thousand years. The sons of Amon were still reigning in Egypt when it was founded."

"And what is this School doing?" I asked.

"We research and study history. There have already been twenty-three dynasties of teachers. But we two have been chosen to leave the borders of our home, as the first and maybe also the last ones."

"But," I inquired, "if you never leave your Sixt Katarakt, how then can you research history?"

"We don't use the same methods as are applied among those of the Evening Countries—or rather, those which *were* used there. The fundaments of those methods were logical conclusions and empirical research: excavations, the study of archives, the deciphering of inscriptions. These sources are deceiving: they can have different explanations, are vague, can be ambiguous and are generally superficial. We try to approach true history along clearer and more secure paths: by looking with the inner, sympathetical senses, using our minds to draw spiritual conclusions, not logical but intuitive ones. In this way a clear, faultless view of whatever happened in world history, forward as well as backward, is shown to the Blessed among us in a series of pure images."

"And why have you finally begun basing your researches on factual dates after all?" I asked, I must say not without a trace of irony in my voice.

"One day—for the first time since the era of our Most Blessed Founder—we found out to our great amazement that our intuitions became disorderly; they flowed into each other and disappeared finally in a foglike grayness. Some mysterious negative power, something alien, hostile and disintegrating had forced its way into the chain of events of history, and threatened to disrupt it. We sensed that it must be somewhere in the north, and we were chosen to begin seeking this power. We have been wandering for two and a half years, but now we have found it."

"And what is it?"

"What else could it be but your Time Machine? It is the greatest unforeseen in the events of history, that which was never seen before and—the Blessed One will excuse my words—that which does not belong in history. It is anti-historical! It makes every historical issue impossible, as the machine has at each moment the possibility to turn each event around, change it, twist and distort, double or postpone it, drown it in absurdity."

"But my Time Machine exists only once, and so does world history! The two just have to get along together."

"That is impossible. There are only two singular solutions possible. Either there is no world history, or there is no Time Machine."

"If this is really so, well, then I am sorry for world history. Because there can be no doubt that my Time Machine exists. Or do you doubt that?"

The Egyptian didn't answer right away. Then he said thoughtfully: "This is a question which can only be solved by an inside look. In any case it would be an extraordinary meeting of circumstances that we arrived here exactly at the same moment as your machine stopped. Extraordinary, and yet when we look in the mirror of a higher possibility it seems understandable, even self-evident."

"But I didn't want to come here at all," I said. "The reason for my arrival was a completely unforeseen and inexplicable accident." I told them about the time-shadow.

The younger Egyptian nodded, and said: "That must have been a Selenite."

"Yes," the older one agreed. "But, indeed, the

Blessed One couldn't foresee this at all. In your time they didn't know yet about the existence of the Moon People. I regret this, but I cannot explain it in detail either because to really understand it, one must possess those faculties which you call 'occult.' But you will understand the reason for the interference immediately.

"The Moon People inhabit the Fourth Dimension. I mean: they have only three dimensions, exactly as we do, but three different ones, and one of those is that dimension which we call the fourth. From this follows that they are able to move in Time, but not—or only very little—in the . . . but this would lead us too far from the subject.

"You have been caught in the time-field of a Selenite, and this was the barrier which stopped your Time Machine. If you would have met another Time Machine, as you thought—though I must say that I have never heard of another one—then you would simply have moved straight through its time-field. The most that could have happened was that your machine would have been slowed down slightly while passing, if you were moving in the other direction. You may be sure that the interfering power was indeed a Selenite. As you know, the moon has a different time than Earth, not a very important difference but just enough to disturb the balance of your machine."

"But if this was the real cause," I said suspiciously, "then it can happen anytime again!"

"Absolutely! But there is a very simple solution to that problem. You have only to use a very high velocity. That way you'll *cut through* the time-field; meaning that you'll move through it so fast that it won't have the time to influence your machine. There was no need at all for you to turn around; it would have been sufficient to move faster. But as we said: it seems it just *had* to be this way, so that you would have to land here."

"But how did *you* come here?" I asked. "You have no vehicles, no materials, not even shoes."

"We don't need such things. I have already explained this to the Most Blessed One: we possess the ability to penetrate into the real insides of anything living, by using our sympathetical senses. By using this insight potential, we can tap even vegetational power, make it into an ally and use it as our servant, just as you by using your calculative intelligence have penetrated into the domain of mineral power. Your method is mechanical, ours is living; our material comes from the organic world, yours from the world of dead things. Your engines are electrical, ours are mental rivers. One little blooming flower contains more enormous and multiple latent powers than a steam engine, only it doesn't respond to the magic of numerals as the dead objects, but rather the magic of the living words."

"You'll excuse me if I can't follow completely," I said, a bit piqued. The profound monologue was beginning to get on my nerves. "You would help me more by having the kindness to tell me how I can get down there. I haven't had breakfast yet, and I'd like to find out if they still don't have beer in London. But of course you don't know what that is, do you?"

"Of course we know what beer is," the Egyptian replied, smiling. "After all, we invented it! But what do you mean by 'getting down there'?"

"Well, into the underground city of London, of course!"

The Egyptian shook his head. "There is no London anymore. It's gone."

"How did that happen to come about?" I asked, horrified.

"Well, the usual way . . . wars . . . revolutions . . . it's always the same thing over and over again. You from the Evening Countries are still young, and so it still terrifies you. Your history has no age, and your age has no history. What other way could there be for your kind of people? Every war creates the seeds of a new revolution, and every revolution starts a new war. Are you interested, though? Well, it started with a discussion about the two Poles. . . ."

"No, don't!" I begged him. "It doesn't interest me at all! If you are going to tell me now everything that happened during the next two hundred years, backward, I might as well hang myself. If I read the last pages of a novel first, as some perverse readers prefer to do, the book loses all its appeal for me. Hope and curiosity are the two big powers which force us to continue our existence in repulsive circumstances. It is exactly our not-knowing that is the thrusting power behind our most daring adventures, the constant source of our action. A man who has seen all the twists and turns of destiny in its complete unity no longer would have the courage to do anything about it. He who *knows* can't act anymore."

"Very wise words indeed," the Egyptian said, "but is there a need to act?"

I continued, however, without paying attention to his words. "Though I don't possess your mysterious intuition, and only have my poorly constructed machine, still I have had a far wider glance into history than you'll ever have. And I'm sorry about it, because what I saw was distasteful, and horrible."

So I told them the things I had seen during my journey to the year 802,000, the report of which has been made public by Mr. Wells: how humanity had finally been split into two species. How the Eloi had reached the highest plane of physical beauty and refinement through a continual existence of idleness, and how their minds had fallen down to near-complete infantilism; while the others, the Morlocks, had developed into apelike underground creatures, mindless work mechanisms, through their uninterrupted manual labor.

The older Egyptian shook his head unbelievingly. "I don't believe this. Life is the power of the Mind, and the Law of the Mind is to reach higher. Throwbacks will always occur, but this is only a superficial death; the Mind breathes and is absorbing power, as an animal which sleeps through the winter. Just look at our own Egypt! As far back as twelve thousand years ago, there existed a giant city situated at the roots of the Delta, which was then much closer to the sea. This was the city of Seth, and from there the Sons of the Gods reigned over the whole of Egypt. The city was destroyed, and many, many metropolises became its mighty descendants. But in between there always were hundreds of years filled with ruins. What you have told us, however, would be something absolute, and definite. I can't accept that."

"Well, then you have the choice: you can call me a madman, or a liar," I exclaimed angrily.

The Egyptian made a respectful bow, his hand at his forehead. "Of course I do not doubt the reality of the impressions of the Most Blessed One," he said softly, "but the impressions of humans . . ."

"May I have the privilege of asking the Favorite of the Gods a question?" the younger one interrupted our conversation. "Do you know absolutely that what you say happened *here?*"

"Where else could it be? My machine travels

only in the dimension of Time! I haven't moved from the same place during those eight hundred thousand years!"

"May I inquire which velocity the Enlightened One used during this time?"

"The strongest one, of course! Else it would have been clearly impossible to move such an enormous time-distance. The highest time-energy my machine is capable of achieving is the time-meter, the three hundred million meter-second, meaning about ten years per second. So even when traveling with maximum velocity, it still took more than twenty-two hours."

The two Egyptians looked at each other, and smiled. Then the younger one said: "If such was the case, then what the Most Blessed One has seen couldn't have been on this Earth. The highest velocity is that of light. From this follows that by moving enormous time-distances, the movement of Time itself, exactly as a ray of light, must finally become a curve. Your journey has brought you to another Earth, an Earth of another time. What you saw there was not an end, but rather a beginning: the creation of two new formidable species of life out of the primitive fundamental childhood stadia. One has been chosen to personify beauty, nobility and goodness; the other to serve duty, labor and progress, and this will finally bring them to the development of one species of pure soul, and one of pure mind! To search for the destiny of our own Earth, you should have traveled along a straight time-line, but then you would have had to travel much more slowly. If we take into account the shortness of a human life, especially since you would have needed a departure and return trip, you wouldn't have gone far. So as you see, the possibilities of your machine are—at least for the future—very limited. I suspect this will be the same for the past also, though the movement barriers for negative times are probably different."

I felt my face turning red. "Now I have absolutely had enough of this nonsense! I have used up all my patience!" I shouted angrily. "First you tell me that my machine has no right to exist at all as it is something which doesn't mesh with world history, and now you are trying to prove that it isn't good for anything at all! Please remember that I did arrive here at our rendezvous much sooner than you did! It took you two and a half years of wandering around, which is more than nine hundred Earth rotations, while I needed maybe at the most one hundredth part of one rotation! Will you gentlemen please do me the courtesy of excusing me? I have other and more important matters to attend to!"

"We are inconsolate for having angered the Friend of the Gods," the two Egyptians said almost at the same moment.

But I had had more than enough of them. With one jump I sat on my machine, pushed the backward-handle and left them. Still, the conceited objections of the Egyptians had already fastened themselves to my subconscious, and involuntarily I started with a very low velocity.

The Egyptians turned transparent, then misty. My last view of the year 2123—as seen through a distorting mist—were the two thin men who were walking reverentially around the place where I had been standing with my Time Machine.

Chapter VIII

The Catastrophe

I felt very angry. Those two barefooted morons, with their idiotic tales of their crazy mind-school where one becomes a historical researcher by sitting down and staring at one's navel; moon-cows throwing time-shadows; buttercups whose power moves engines; and finally even trying to curve Time! My anger was only intensified by the dark premonition that maybe in one way or another they had been right. Because it was true that light doesn't move in a straight-line direction over long distances, and if the origin of that was indeed the high velocity, then indeed this could be true of Time also. I made the decision to think it over in more detail at a better suited time.

Easily I wandered along. The several changes of air hadn't been working to my advantage. Just as the atmosphere in 1995 had been too poor in ozone, now I had had too much of it for my taste. I felt slightly drugged by the narcotic scents of the giant plants, almost as much as by the confusing double-talk of the Egyptians. My spirit of enterprise, however, was only increased by the constant obstacles placed in my way.

My original plan to journey to the year 1840 suddenly seemed rather bourgeois and stupid to

me. The least I could do now with the time-energy
I had accumulated seemed a venture into the time
when Atlantis was still a leading culture. This would
at most be a matter of twenty thousand, maybe even
only fifteen thousand years. What kinds of buildings
would have stood here at that time? Maybe one of
those ten thousand towers built of gold-brass ore as
described by Plato, with trumpeting hordes of
elephants in coats of mail all around them. Maybe
there was just another war or revolution going on!
Always the same!

I must say that those two bronze skins had really
succeeded in destroying my pleasure in world history. But precisely through their words, which still
echoed in my mind, I suddenly got hold of an absolutely titantic idea: I decided to find out the truth
about *Time* itself.

I would journey down into the past of Earth—
even if the movement of Time made a curve—
through the millions and billions of years of its
creation period, till I reached the Earth in gaseous
form, and then beyond till I would arrive where
there was no Earth left, not even an Earth of
"another time." What would I find there? There
was the key to the mystery of Time. Because my
machine—as long as it traveled in the past or the
future of Earth—was still a machine of this Earth:
it possessed Earth-Time, even when multiplied a
million times.

If, however, the Earth had disappeared . . . what
Time would the machine have then? I would finally
meet a zone of free Time, absolute pure Time,
abstract Time, the real essence of Time itself. The
whole idea of course was the result of the narcotic
influence of the alien plants' scents of the Egyptian's
time. Because it really was an insane idea, wasn't

it? But don't worry: I didn't get that far . . . not by a long shot!

During my journey, London suddenly reappeared in the sky, so it must have disappeared—must disappear?—in a sudden catastrophe. It stood there majestically for a long time on its fundaments of clouds. Then the imposing towers and housing blocks began to lose one floor after another, till they finally were all gone. At the same time giant masses of metal and stone grew out of the earth, putting the good old down-to-earth London together again. At first they were overarched by gigantic air constructions: buildings over a hundred stories, elastic floating bridges and freewalks in between; however, as time ran backward, the city began to crouch down and its general view became more familiar.

I was approaching my own time: the year 1911 was already passing. I must admit that I had a few doubts concerning the exact date of my start. There was always the possibility that something horrible would happen as I passed this point, some borderline accident which I couldn't have foreseen. I slowed down my velocity, but the pointer was moving relentlessly: now it was showing November 1905. For a fraction of a second I had a glimpse of the fiery bronze hair of Gloria as I moved through the seventh of May. She was still sitting in the same unmoving posture I had left her in. Calculating in Earth-Time this meant hours. She had been waiting there so long! Before I had the time to think about this, however, the pointer stood at the fourth of May.

The machine made a slight jump, as a wheel passing over a high stone, then it continued. The passage had succeeded! The past was conquered, its immense empire was open to me!

I had sobered, breathing in the normal air, and I was now in the best of spirits. In fact, I should have made a short stop at Miss Gloria, I said to myself; I had promised it to her after all. But I didn't want to give just a partial first report, rather the account of my whole journey. Yet God knew how long that would last, and she had been waiting a long time already. But after all there was no need to keep her waiting: I could stop at whatever moment I wished. When I returned, I just had to journey to the seventh of May, and stop there. But I had seen that she had already been waiting for hours. How was that possible? If I . . .

At that moment I was hit by a sudden gush of wind. I felt myself being lifted off the machine and was thrown with my back against something hard. A fizzling sound, which changed into a roar, hit my ears, and a freezing cold ran through my body. At the same time complete darkness descended over me, and I lost consciousness.

Chapter IX

A Winter Night During a Morning in May

The Time Traveler took a few puffs of his pipe. "Don't you think," he continued his narrative, "that this is in fact a very unclear and untruthful expression: 'to lose consciousness'? In my opinion one can lose everything, except consciousness. Someone in a state of narcosis is said to be unconscious. However, they live through anything possible, give long monologues and are able to play long parts. I would say that consciousness is needed for that! Furthermore, all acknowledged psychologists assure us that there is no such thing as a dreamless sleep: so even while sleeping, consciousness never leaves us. It is also said of people who are in the grip of high emotional upheavals such as anger, fear, love and madness that they are out of their minds. However, while in these emotional states they often execute actions of an extremely refined suitability. The same is true of people under hypnosis: they act absolutely intelligently, so they must be conscious. Also a drunkard: the things he says and does very often have a definite metaphysical nature. Now let's have a look at the other side of the coin: even when we're sober, the highest number of images or ideas which we can hold at one time in our minds is about ten; as soon as an eleventh appears, the first disappears. And yet it isn't lost, else it couldn't return. The container holding it is our consciousness.

"So the consciousness is always present: while under the influence of drugs, while 'unconscious,' in a trance, apparently dead, yes, even after death. Death itself is nothing else but a form of narcosis in which one doesn't speak, a sleep which is falsely said to be dreamless. From this we can come to the conclusion that the consciousness must even have been present before birth, because . . ."

"I admit that these are very original and interesting aspects about which you are talking," I said, moving back and forth on my chair, " but I would be even more interested to learn the explanation of the accident with your Time Machine. Why did you get thrown out of the seat? Why did everything become dark?"

"But I am telling you," the Time Traveler said. "Just let me explain it all in chronological order. First of all, I have to explain to you how it is possible that I lost consciousness and yet couldn't lose it."

"And when you awoke, what happened then?"

"Again a wrong expression. One is always awake!"

"All right, when that which we wrongly call 're-gaining consciousness' happened to you, what occurred then?"

Here the Time Traveler took on a trance-like appearance once more and returned to his narration, almost as if I no longer existed in the same time-plane as he did.

The first thing I noticed was a painful bump on the back of my head, which I literally felt swelling under my fingers. Slowly my eyes adapted to the darkness, and then I could see that I was lying on the ground in my garden, next to my house. The earth felt hard as stone and was icy cold. It was in the middle of night. A howling gush of wind was shaking the naked trees, and angry clouds of thick hailstones mixed with snow were coming down in torrents, whipping my face. I was wet through and through.

With difficulty I rose and stumbled into my rooms. Of course I had no matches in my pockets, and I had to search for them, but finally I was able to turn on the lights. I went to the fireplace, and discovered to my astonishment that the logs were already blazing, spreading an enjoyable warmth. What had happened here? Were there goblins at work?

I looked around. My writing-room hadn't changed at all, but it was unexplainable how I had got here. I hadn't stopped the machine. Or had my machine stopped by its own power? But where was the machine? Only now I realized that in my initial confusion I hadn't even bothered to look at my machine. I opened a window and looked out, down to my garden. But I couldn't see the machine!

I ran down like a madman and began searching everywhere, without result: the machine was not to be found. Deeply depressed, I returned to my room. A new storm wind had gotten hold of the open windows, and spread them inside my room into a thousand shards of glass. Hailstones were dancing on my carpet.

I closed the wooden blinds, and began thinking it over. Whatever had happened? Had the resistance of Earth-Time proven unconquerable after all? It could be that its interfering power had been working at full force only one day later—or earlier—on the third of May, instead of on the fourth. But why the

explosion and the fall? Had the explosion been the
unforeseen result of the collision of two times at
war with each other? But this was clear nonsense,
a collision is only possible between objects in three
dimensions, and whatever had happened, had been
in the one and only Time Dimension.

Even if I accepted that the impossible had happened after all, I still should have found the pieces
of my exploded machine. But there was not a single
piece to be found, not a single gear wheel, not the
slightest trace of its existence. It had disappeared like
a ghost. And outside there was a snowstorm and torrents of hailstones, on the third of May!

Even worse, it was the deepest of night when it
should have been morning! You see, the smallest
time-unit my machine possesses is one day. This
is a very little unit, as one day isn't even the three
and a half thousandth part of a time-meter. So the
only time at which I could have landed was shortly
after half past nine in the morning, because that's
the time I left the Egyptians.

While brooding over it, I lit a cigarette—something which I only do, as you know well enough,
while in an absolutely foul temper. Was it possible
that I had really dreamed it all: the sweet sea-
eyed Gloria, the projected man of Savory & Com-
pany, the violet dragonflowers and the mad Egyptians? Maybe my whole adventure had been only a
grog fantasy, and I hadn't been away at all in reality!

But a long chain of evidence proved the contrary:
lamplight instead of the morning sun, a red-tongued
fire instead of a blue sky in May, and a howling
storm instead of the soft spring air. I felt, saw and
heard all these changes with my senses, which now
were alert and very sober. I felt the ice-cold wind
coming in through gaps in the shutters, I heard

the downpour of hailstones, and the howling of the storm, I saw the water and the glass shards on my carpet, and most important and most sad of all: what I did *not* see was my machine. Where was it?

I had calmed down a bit, and now tried to reach a logical conclusion, by using rational observations. One thing was certain: through the interference of some unknown force I had not conquered the resistance of Earth-Time, because now I was here in my own room, and only one day in the past. This still did not explain the fatal disappearance of my machine. If the resistance of Earth-Time was really unconquerable, then my machine should have stopped, and that would have been all. And where did this absolute darkness come from? This phenomenon had nothing at all to do with the resistance of Earth-Time. And what about the storm?

And here I suddenly had a thought . . . if you can call it so. Maybe my violent catastrophe with the machine had occurred precisely because of the sudden change of the weather. Because what is "weather"? A phenomenon of Time! If everything is going fine, they say *schöne Zeit, beau temps, bel tempo* . . . literally "good time"! The unexplainable appearance of night could be an eclipse of the sun. Without a sun there is no time, thus also no Time Machine, so it had disappeared for the time being. Of course this was all a potpourri of pure nonsense. There hadn't been an eclipse of the sun on the third of May. And a special delivery storm of my own making was also very improbable. But if you had been in my strained condition, you wouldn't have found more satisfactory reasons either.

I closed the front door and mechanically went to get the paper from the mailbox. It was the *Sunday Times*. Strange, the third of May hadn't been a Sunday at all. Short story, a horrible choice, "What we would like to get from Santa Claus." Really, this kind of rubbish the editor could have saved till the sixth of December! Or maybe it was a leftover from last Christmas? Theater and arts: "The premiere of Pinero's newest comedy *Sinchen's Mystery* will take place next week at the Haymarket Theater." But that piece was already a public scandal! "The rehearsals for the Christmas plays have been started at the Strand Theater." Why in the Devil's name should they rehearse Christmas plays in May?

News from the fronts: "Since the battle of Schaho position warfare is being kept up through the country. Port Arthur is besieged. After ten days of continuing attacks, the 'High Mountain,' the front defense at the northwest side of the city has been evacuated. General Kondratenko has watched over the defense, but one can still expect the definite fall of the fortress within a few months, maybe even within a few weeks if the Russians don't succeed in bringing reinforcements to the city." But this was absurd: the Russian-Japanese War had been over and done with for some time! What kind of paper was this?

How stupid of me! I had taken an old issue from the sixth of December. But why was it still in its delivery envelope? My wandering gaze fell on the weather report: "Since yesterday London has been in the grip of weather conditions which even in December have been scarce: snowstorms, mixed with rain and winds resembling a miniature tornado. . . ." Weird, this was exactly the kind of weather which it was now. . . .

And suddenly I thought I understood it all. I couldn't be at the third of May at all, I was really at the sixth of December! Being occupied with my thoughts I mustn't have paid attention to the fact that I had slipped further. Maybe I had even accidentally touched the handle myself, and quickened my velocity. But all of this still offered no reasonable explanation for the sudden halt of my machine, and especially its mysterious disappearance. The machine should be here, it was after all *in* Time, in any time, within a thousand years as well as before a thousand years, tomorrow and the day after tomorrow as well as yesterday and the day before that.

At that moment I nearly fainted. Because in one sudden flash I understood the whole terrible truth.

Chapter X

Two Times Burgundy

Through his excitement, the Time Traveler had forgotten his pipe, and he now lit it again, while continuing in a dull voice: "You will agree that my situation was really dreadful, one of the most appalling and horrible situations imaginable. Since the world exists, no human has ever found himself caught in such a predicament, and I sincerely hope no one ever will again. I had had the good fortune to escape all the dangers threatening my journey: the resistance of Earth-Time, the cathodic rays of the radiodrom, the time-shadow of the Selenite, the fall from two stories' height, but this obstacle couldn't be conquered." He became mute, staring moodily into space.

"But I don't see why," I said uncertainly.

"Don't you understand it at all?" he exclaimed. "The case was damned clear. I had journeyed into a time when my machine hadn't been invented yet! How is it possible that I—who call myself a scientifically thinking person—hadn't thought about this primitive fact! I could hardly travel with my Time Machine to a time when it didn't exist! Now you'll smile, and probably I would have done so myself, if the matter hadn't been so vital to me. . . ."

Again there was a silence. The Time Traveler was speechless, sending clouds of smoke into the air.

I said: "I understand that. But the story doesn't fit. When did you finish your Time Machine?"

"I couldn't tell you the exact date, but it was somewhere in the middle of January."

"Well, then! Your machine should have disappeared in the middle of January, and you would have been shipwrecked—or rather machinewrecked—there, and not on the sixth of December. And your situation wouldn't have been so desperate at all, because your machine should have given up at the exact moment when it lacked one single rod or screw. The rest would have been intact. So the only thing you would have had to do was to finish the near-complete machine by adding the lacking rod or screw on the fourteenth of January or whenever it was. Then you could have traveled forward in the functioning machine to our own time."

"Yes," the Time Traveler said, "one would suppose so. But after having thought about it for a long while, I found out that it wasn't that way at all. My machine had conquered the resistance of Earth-Time . . . it had conquered that resistance too well! Being an Earth machine, it was subject to the law of inertia. During my journeys it had been accumulating energy, so when it finally broke down, it still continued its way for a short time period, due to that law. That's why I arrived during the night, when I had started in the morning. A catastrophe doesn't submit itself to my time-meter and its gradations. Sometime during the millionth part of a time-meter the amount of energy was diminished and the movement was put to an abrupt halt. In a way even in my misfortune I had been lucky: if I hadn't been traveling so slowly at the moment when the catastrophe happened, if I had been traveling at a higher or maybe even the highest velocity of my machine, I would have been thrown much farther backward, perhaps into the time of Mr. Carlyle or the time-era of Queen Anne. Then my predicament would really have been hopeless, and we would never have seen each other again."

"I don't see the difference," I said. "Once your machine was gone, it wouldn't matter if you had lost it during the time of the Spanish succession wars or during the Russian-Japanese Wars."

"I will explain that later. By the way, most of the time I was thinking along the same lines as you are now, that's why I hadn't the smallest hope left. Just try to imagine it: I was chained forever to the evening of the sixth of December in Nineteen-Four!" he said angrily.

I didn't quite know what to say to that. "Maybe if it still irritates you so much, you'd prefer to tell the rest another time," I stammered, "or at least take a glass of whisky and soda."

"No," he rejected, "only soda, without whisky. It will calm me." He drank eagerly. "So, now we can continue. I puzzled my head for a long time, but it was impossible to hold a clear thought. Also, I felt absolutely exhausted after the many agitating experiences I had been through. I fell down on my bed, and slept uneasily.

"When I awoke, I had real difficulties in piecing the whole thing together again. The closed window shutters, the downpouring hail, the *Sunday Times*: it was all still there. Even the light was still burning: now in a way it had become a kind of Eternal Light. But the rest had done me a lot of good, and my mind felt considerably clearer and refreshed, so much so in fact that I began to look for a way to get help. The first thing was to try to find a way of communication between myself and the present: I mean between my and your present.

After having thought about it for a long time, I finally decided to try the wireless telegraph. As you know, an electric spark has the same velocity as light: three hundred thousand kilometers in one second. So the spark moves more than six hundred thousand times as quickly as the Earth, needing less than one six hundred thousandth of a second for one day. So, using this vehicle, I could easily cover the time-span of five months which was between your and my time; it would only be a matter of a four thousandth of one second.

"So I sent you the first telegram. I admit it was a bit short and confusing, but I could hardly explain it all to you in detail at the time: such long telegrams aren't practical, and I suppose you wouldn't have understood it all anyway. But the most important things could be communicated by this means. Of course one thing couldn't be helped: it had to remain a one-way communication. You couldn't send telegrams to me: it is impossible to turn back the movement of electrical energy, its only direction is forward.

"I had a definite aim, at which I would concentrate all my efforts: I had to find a way to reconstruct my machine. But where to start? First of all I didn't have the complicated calculations I had needed to build the machine. These I could reconstruct, even if it took me years; but there were a few very important formulas which I had only discovered near the end of December, and these I had forgotten completely. And I especially needed radium, and where could I obtain it?

"Within one day—but that is a misleading statement: to me there existed *only one* day!—I found a valuable ally, which unforgivably I hadn't thought

of before. It was the little Time Machine. Not only
was this a priceless model for the construction of the
big machine, but it could also travel through Time
by its own power. Suddenly I had discovered the
means for a two-way communication, and even
for transport! So I sent you the machine with the
included message, which you got. With this small
vehicle I could hope to receive all I needed, if I had
enough patience. I felt much better already!"

"But why did you send me such angry telegrams?"

"Because the little machine never arrived!"

"But I addressed it quite correctly!"

"I know," the Time Traveler said, "and exactly
because you had addressed it so correctly . . . I don't
blame you, of course. It wasn't your fault at all,
but mine, or rather the fault of the situation. But
I couldn't explain it then and of course I was absolutely furious at you. I believe I even sent you something about a hippopotamus."

"No," I said, "it was a rhinoceros you compared
me with. But that doesn't matter."

"I kept on thinking and puzzling till I thought my
head would burst," the Time Traveler continued,
"but I didn't find a solution. Maybe, I thought at
first, it was because I hadn't mentioned the exact
time of the day. But that couldn't be the cause.
Knowing your obligingness and your reliability—
please, don't bother, it isn't a compliment—I was
certain that you would execute what I had asked
you as soon as possible. So the little machine would
arrive about eleven A.M. This wasn't quite the exact
time, but that didn't mean a thing, because then it
would be here at least by evening. It might have
been bad if you'd taken your time, say till late in
the night. But I didn't expect that, especially since
I had explicitly demanded you to do what I asked in
a hurry."

"I dispatched the machine at ten thirty-nine."

"Well, you see!" The Time Traveler nodded. "But then I remembered the resistance of Earth-Time. Just as the big machine, the little one had to conquer that. But of course you couldn't know anything about that, and so it seemed the little machine had given up on the way back to me. Indeed, if you had known about Earth-Time and the only means to conquer it, it still would have been impossible, because though you would have been able to send the little machine into the future, you couldn't travel with it and direct it back to the past. After thinking it over, however, I recognized that this solution wouldn't work out either. After all I had dispatched the machine into the future myself, and when it arrived in your time it had already accumulated the time-energy of five months, or one hundred and fifty times Earth-Time.

"Although the reason was unknown, the result was clear enough: no calculation tables, no materials, and then I lost the irreplaceable scale model too. The final hope for returning to my own time seemed cut off. I resigned myself to my fate.

"It is a very bizarre situation when Time has stopped moving. There are no hopes left, but also no fears. No tensions, no worries, including worries about food. At that time I was working on the final theoretical formulas needed for the building of my big machine. Whenever I'm like that, fully occupied with something I feel compelled to finish, I have the habit of literally barricading myself in my own house so that no one can come and disturb me at my work. Almost as if preparing myself for a siege, I had bought quite a provision of wood, tobacco, tins of food, beer, Dutch rusks and similar things.

"Outside it remained an unbearably stormy winter night, so I never opened the window shutters. In

the long run this could have become unpleasant, but
fortunately a few months before I had installed an
excellent new ventilator, which completely satisfied
my thirst for fresh air. The continuing life under
artificial light, however, did get on my nerves. I
really am a 'Friend of the Sun' as those two madmen
of the Nile preferred to call me; you know that I
always get sick at masked balls and evening parties;
you have laughed at me often enough for that.

"Anyway, I did find something to console me. For
example, in the lowest shelf of a bookcase, next to
Frazer's *Dictionary of Practical Chemistry,* I found
a whole case of Romanée, Pommard and Nuits. It
is a really satisfying pleasure to drink one's own
burgundy twice. Also there were the six bottles of
Canadian Club Whisky; you'll remember the one
that tasted like very old cognac. And the reborn
lobster salad of Cross & Blackwell wasn't bad either.

"On the whole, my situation was nothing less than
comic! Just think about it: a man without a future!
I thought about myself as a modern 'Peter Schlemil':
a man without a shadow.* Because we humans
throw our shadows forward, but never backward.
'Mankind,' Emerson says, 'is a walking prophecy
of the future.' But before me was nothing but a
black wall. I had risked taking too much time for
myself, and now I was convicted to spend the rest
of my life without time, because I had lost the past
also. There is no past without a future.

"Continuously mulling over such thoughts can
only lead to insanity, so I began searching for ways
to distract my mind. At first the burgundy proved a
great help. A mysterious drink it is: fiery yet leaden,
it gives one wings and puts one down at the same

*"Peter Schlemil"—German idiom, meaning a patient un-
lucky fellow.

time. I stayed in a mild drunken state for a long time; I suppose I even still look a bit like it. But in my situation anyone would have taken to the bottle.

"Then I began seeking comfort in books, but not in the technical works which till then had been my principal reading matter. Science had lost its appeal and glamour for me; I never even set foot in my laboratory. The strongest consolation I found was in an ancient collection of mystical works, which I had inherited from my father and had never looked at before. The most beautiful proved to be the words of Master Eckhart, which seemed as if written directly to me: 'It is all only a *now*.' I had to think about the legend of the Monk of Heisterbach, who walked through a thousand years in one day, because it makes no difference to God: 'To Him one day is as a thousand years, and a thousand years are as one day to him.'

"And isn't it exactly like that? What is our existence but a quarter of an hour rainbow, a ribbon of light between two eternities? Does the soul, when it lives a hundred years, more closely approach eternity than if it existed for only one day? Why would it be impossible for a wise man who has *really lived* for one day by patiently and intently listening to his soul, to learn more about the pulse of eternity than we'll ever be able to understand on this material world? This crystalline 'eternal *now*' in which I was caught, wasn't this in fact the most sublime situation, the most worthy place for a true human? But it was too big, too sublime for a weak human!

"And I spoke aloud to myself: 'Time stands still.' And I listened attentively to its silence.

"At this moment I had a terrible scare. My ears had been sharpened by the constant unchanging silence, and now I heard a clock ticking, very softly but absolutely clearly. A clock in my house! It was almost a ghostly answer to my words. So Time wasn't standing still. The sound came from above. One second I stood there as if petrified, then I was running, jumping two, three steps up the stairs."

Chapter XI

The Time Traveler Returns

"As I tore open the door of my laboratory, I nearly fainted. I was thrown back almost bodily by what I saw. It was full day! Outside it was a joyful windless winter morning, snow was glittering on the trees. The ticking clock showed eleven a.m. and the second hand was moving. I looked at the tear calendar: it showed the fifth of February. Still dazed, I went to the tower room: there the calendar in the corner read the thirty-first of December. A strange confusion indeed! Below it was night, here above it was morning; in my writing-room it was one day, in my laboratory another, and in the tower room yet a third.

"I glanced at the other corner. And there I saw something which nearly drove me insane with joy. There it was standing, sparkling in the morning light, complete and sound . . . my Time Machine! I could have kissed and hugged it! I didn't stop and wonder how it was possible for the thing to climb two floors high along the wall of my house. I climbed into it, and for the first and the last time I used it for a sensible purpose: I journeyed back to my own time.

"So, that is my story."

"Please excuse me," I said, "but that is not the

whole story. You still haven't told me how you got your machine back."

"Well, it really surprises me that you haven't figured it out on your own! I can understand that I hadn't thought of it, after all I was quite depressed and half insane. But you shouldn't have forgotten the phenomenon every child knows: we grow older. Every man each day covers a specific time-distance: one day. When someone has covered a time-span of twenty years (two time-meters) we say that he is twenty years 'old,' then thirty, and so on. When someone has covered two years of time more than someone else, then we say that he is two years 'older,' and if that second person himself has covered two years we say again that he is two years 'older.' It is ridiculously simple.

Now I myself had grown one Earth-day older each day, and so had slowly approached. That means: I could not conquer the distance to my own time, which remained constant. With every day that I grew older, my own time also moved one day forward and away from me, so the distance never lessened. But I could gain on my Time Machine, because only six weeks separated me from its completion. If I would have been traveling with a higher velocity at the moment of the catastrophe, I would have been thrown farther back and would have had to wait longer to catch up with the machine. So it was absolutely not the same if I landed in December 1904 or in the era of Queen Anne, as you took for granted before. If that would have been the case, I would have had to grow two hundred years older before I would have arrived at my Time Machine."

"But you said you'd finished your machine in the middle of January. Then why was the calendar in the laboratory showing the fifth of February and in the tower room the thirty-first of December?"

"This too can be explained very simply. The calendar in the tower room was a dated calendar, which I simply had forgotten to renew after the end of the year 1904. But the date in the laboratory was exact: it was really the fifth of February. Because only on that date did I enter that room. I had been waiting more than three weeks too long in what I thought was the sixth of December. If I had checked the laboratory at regular intervals, I could have spared myself this overtime. I could have especially spared myself my deep despair, since I would have noticed immediately that my adventures were limited in time to about forty days. This way, however, it had turned into sixty-one days.

"My time stopped at the fourth of July, and to reach this I only needed the short trip covering one hundred and forty-nine days, which is the distance that had been created by the catastrophe. As I said, I've been here since the day before yesterday, but I really didn't need any comfort!"

"Now I understand at last," I added ardently, "why the little Time Machine didn't reach its destination though it was correctly addressed. Because it was also wrongly addressed! When your telegram arrived, it was the tenth of May. So I should have sent the machine to the twelfth of December, not to the sixth, because you were already in the twelfth then!"

"Indeed." The Time Traveler nodded. "That's how it was, and as I said, you can't be blamed at all!"

"But neither can you!" I exclaimed angrily. "The only blame is on the part of humanity's backwardness. Why didn't Stephenson invent the time horse at the same time as the iron horse? And why didn't

Marconi find out how to send wireless telegrams into the past as well? Negative electricity exists so . . ."

The Time Traveler stopped me. "That's all over now," he said, and then added with a little resigned smile, "But I made a small discovery after all. It is possible to take moving pictures with a camera, while moving very slowly with the Time Machine."

"Now don't get angry," I replied, "but there's hardly need for a Time Machine for that. The Lumière brothers made a similar invention many years ago."

"But I'm sure that the results obtained through the use of my Time Machine are incomparably better."

"Absolutely, but what use would one have for such time pictures? For scientific means, this method has already been used for years; I read about it not so long ago in a professional biology journal. And I don't think that the public is interested in such photo-mechanical experiments."

"Well, it hardly matters," the Time Traveler said tiredly. "In any case, an embarrassing disgrace is all that is left of the experiment. Again science has ended in a miserable fiasco. I know one thing for certain: I'll never use the damned thing again. Neither in the past, nor in the future. What is worth searching for there? Supercivilization or barbarism! Savory idiots and Katarakt idiots! Besides, this whole 'exploration impulse of the researcher' is in fact an absolute absurdity, a big laugh! No matter if one tries to conquer the Earth, Space, Time or any other dimension, one always neglects the one and only conquest worth the trouble, in fact the only one possible: one's own 'I.' "

"Excuse me," I said, "but didn't you mention

something in this vein this very evening? Or rather no, it was Miss Gloria."

"That's possible," the Time Traveler said, and covered himself in clouds of smoke.

The End:

A Related Correspondence

1

Mr. Anthony Transic, London ⬥

. . . and so I don't need to mention again how obliged I am, how deeply thankful. Still, there are a few points the clarification of which I have been unable to find in your explanation. I would like to ask you please not to feel angered with me, if I dare pose you a few final questions, having found the courage for this by your great kindness.

First: it is quite clear why Mr. Morton's machine didn't function at his start on the fourth of May, 1905. It is also clear why it did function for his return journeys from the years 1995 and 2123. However, I don't see why it refused on the seventh of May, because then it already had a certain impetus, it had accumulated sufficient energy to conquer the resistance.

Secondly: the Time Traveler stated that he would not mount his machine again, but almost three years have passed, and it looks as if he has changed his mind since then. After all, Time is powerful, even the snail's pace of our trifling Earth-Time. It would be a real pity if Mr. Morton didn't use his machine for small-scale expeditions, after all the machine proved its excellence for small trips to the future. I have a very strong suspicion that he is on one of those at this very moment. Because what else would "Gone on a Journey" mean in his case? I don't think him the type of man who would go to a congress of nature lovers or on a lion's hunt.

Thirdly—but this is in fact a more private matter —whatever became of Miss Gloria? Did those two "find each other" as one used to say?

I would have liked to be able to present you with some interesting news from Vienna, but I can't find anything worth mentioning. The Kaiser still takes a glass of sour milk for breakfast and half of a chicken for dinner. The parliament is still occupied with the language question in Böhm. The city's theaters are still showing melodramas. Peter Altenberg now wears sandals. I think that is about all, so you'll have to be satisfied with my kindest regards.

Sincerely yours,
Friedell.

2

Mr. Egon Friedell, Vienna.

Dear Sir,

Once again your first question shows a deep involvement and lively interest in the case of the Time Machine. It is a pleasure answering this. Mr. Morton as a matter of fact has made one of those stupid little errors which even the greatest scientists often make. In calculating Earth-Time he had divided *s* by *t*: 40,000 kilometers by 86,400 seconds, which gave him as a result less than half a kilometer-second. What he had completely overlooked, however, was that the Earth creates a significantly greater amount of time-energy. The Earth does not turn exclusively on its own axis, but also around the sun covering 365¼ days and 936 million kilometers, almost thirty kilometers each second. Of course, all this is only a ten-thousandth part of one time-meter, but taken as a whole 29,710 meters plus 463 meters (the time-energy of the axis rotation which must be added, of course), so 30,173 meters in one second; it is 65 1/6 times as much as the energy quantum which Mr. Morton had thought of. So his starting velocity was much too low. Instinctively, Gloria had been correct when she advised him to just travel on.

However, concerning Miss Gloria, your request for information also is correct: this is a very private matter. What's more, what in fact do you want? I'm sending you a scientific report of an expedition, and you want a love story with a happy ending! I give you information about calculations and formulas which fit (or sometimes don't), and you expect something along the lines of "boy meets girl"! I have the impression that to be really agreeable to you people in Vienna, every tale should end with a *G'spässie:* I think that is what you call a flirt, or so Laura has told me. She was born in Dresden, but has mastered the famous Viennese dialect very well. Incidentally, Gloria and the Time Traveler were married. Of course.

And here you have at the same time the answer to your third question: at the moment Mr. Morton is on the most mundane and yet most interesting of all journeys: on his honeymoon. Now he is exploring—as your nutty Peter Altenberg would say—the sea-eyes of his young wife. How did they get together and get married? Well, that in fact is really a romance. But don't expect this from me. I have the same opinion about novels as Mr. Wells.

Yours respectfully,
Transic.

Epilogue:

How Should a Gentleman Behave in Such a Case?

Twenty-seven years have passed since my correspondence, and I had nearly forgotten the Time Traveler, the Time Machine, Mr. Transic and his strange report. Then one day, while I was leafing through some old class-books, my glance fell on the manuscript, and I suddenly got the idea that maybe it should be made public after all. It was in fact still a not uninteresting insight about the adventures of an original explorer and his daring experiments. Science can always learn something, even from failures. Mr. Morton's journey into the past is worthy of attention, especially to those who don't object to the sober and often almost wooden description of the adventure which after all is a scientific treatment. They may even find much more solid enjoyment—while learning something—in his report than in many artificial fantasy-images out of the mind of a "poet," which contain nothing more concrete than the unrestrained absurdity of his imagination. At this point I have to agree with the intolerable Miss Hamilton.

The unorthodox form hardly seems an important objection. It is true that the good Mr. Transic is hardly a gifted reporter, far from a good story-teller! Neither is the report of Mr. Morton a soundly constructed and literately finished story, but the often confusing monologue of a specialist thinking with fixed ideas. The Time Traveler, however, and Mr. Transic have one virtue in common which gives them an advantage over many good tale-spinners who are capable of holding their audience in breath-less suspense: they do not cut anything from or add anything to their report; they do not change or camouflage anything. This should be more than sufficient to the reader. And those who don't think this is dramatic enough should go to the movies.

But do I have the right to publish such facts which after all will bring some serious-minded, noble persons into the spotlight, and not always at their best?

Of all those concerned, I think that Mr. Wells deserves the least consideration, and this for several reasons. First of all he ordered Miss Hamilton to write that first rude letter.

Secondly, he has written a *World History* in three volumes, and I have written a *Culture History* in three volumes. Hereupon an English critic has called me the German Wells. Now, when Mr. Wells read this—and people who have had something printed read everything which is printed about them, even if they swear to the contrary—he felt rather hostile toward this insolent critic. Though I had nothing to do with this comparison personally, which was after all an unwanted and undesired event, still I feel certain that Mr. Wells now has a grudge against me too. Moreover, the German translation of his history book is very poor, while the English transla-tion of my book on culture is excellent, so good in fact that I have been thinking of retranslating this edition into German. All this may have angered him too. So I don't think it matters very much if I give him still another reason to resent me.

Thirdly and finally, Mr. Wells was ambitious to write a history "by a layman for laymen," and so have I. I believe that the enormous lack of interest in the history of culture exists mainly because until now books about it were written only by culture-historians. Now, however, there exists not the slightest doubt—I'm not jealous, and I am objective enough to admit this—that Mr. Wells' history book is even less scientific than my own. Though I have honestly tried to make mine as simple and straightforward as possible, still it is much more professional and businesslike than Mr. Wells' book. Therefore his book has had much more success. So Mr. Wells is my triumphant rival in the very limited, specialized field of nonprofessional history writing. I don't think he has any right to a privileged treatment.

Besides, we are living in a very skeptical age. No doubt many people will consider the whole thing a ridiculous joke or an amusing story, and nothing more. They will claim that Mr. Morton never could have seen London in the sky, because the only things they have ever seen there were illuminated advertisements for chocolates and shoe polish. They will maintain that there can be no such things as Selenites, because they haven't yet herded moon-cows with them; and that it is impossible to drink the same sixty bottles of burgundy twice, because they themselves haven't even managed this one time. Even the opinions of those who would believe in his Time Machine won't interest Mr. Morton, because after all he isn't making any more journeys in Time.

But let's be honest: confidential information should stay confidential, even when it has outlived the man, and compromising disclosures shouldn't be made by a gentleman, not even when they are about things which happened a long time ago. Even the probability, rather the certainty, that they wouldn't be believed anyway, still doesn't give one the right of disclosure. It is enough that he himself believes them.

Such excuses could only be given to a professional historian. He could justify himself by proclaiming that the research into long-forgotten experiments is his profession, and that the results of his diggings will only be made known to his colleagues. The more's the pity that I'm not a historian!

THE END

DAW PRESENTS MARION ZIMMER BRADLEY